Copyright © 2017 by Eddie Cleveland
All rights reserved. No part of this book may be reproduced in any form or by any electronic or mechanical means, including information storage and retrieval systems, without written permission from the author, except for the use of brief quotations in a book review.

CHAPTER 1

Holly

I'm straddling Knox's leg. The firm muscles of his thigh are wedged between mine, pressed up against my pussy. The fabric of my short skirt is hiked up, giving a glimpse of my lace thong to the guys – that's how Knox likes it. He likes putting me on display.

I watch the guys. Watch as their eyes dart back and forth from between my thighs to the gun casually resting on Knox's other leg. As if their animal brains are too stupid to decide what to focus on: my panties or the threat of death.

Men.

I'm bored. It's taking all of my self-restraint not to show it. I remember when this used to make me wet. When Knox went through his speech with a new guy about how much coke to sell he would start him off with. When he laid out all of his payment demands, with me on his leg, his coke queen, fuck, I'd practically cum.

Being with one of the most dangerous and powerful drug runners in Miami had a lot of appeal to a messed up seventeen-year-old. And the nights where it lost its lustre, the free-flowing mountains of cocaine never did.

Now, at twenty-two, I've seen it all a million times. I know I'm not Knox's queen; I'm his puppet.

His dummy.

"Since yer new, I'll start ya with four ounces," Knox juts out his jaw and gives a curt nod toward the compact, tinfoil-wrapped brick on the coffee table.

The new guy, Jim, doesn't move. He doesn't blink his icy blue eyes. "I want ten," his lips are tight as the words squeeze between them.

"You got shit in your ears? Or just shit for brains?" Knox's muscles tighten, pushing me up a bit taller. Nobody contradicts Knox. I'm surprised Jim doesn't know that. Or he just doesn't care.

Tommy rests his hand on the new guy's knee, silently instructing him to shut up. "He's starting you with four. End of story, man." Tommy glares into Jim's face.

I can't help but stare into his face too, but not for the same reason. I'm just shocked that someone has the balls to talk back to Knox. It's stupid and it's… kinda hot.

Tommy's greasy helmet of hair doesn't move as he directs his gaze back to meet Knox. "Four is fine, man. Ain't it, Jim?" He prods the man he's vouched for.

"No."

Tommy's eyes squint, causing the three black tears inked onto the outside corner of his eye to crinkle up. Three tears for three lives he's taken. It's a pretty standard prison tat. I try to imagine what Knox's face would look like if he had a tear for every life he snuffed out. The side of his face would be stained black. Just like his soul.

I can feel Knox's rage seething from his pores. I don't need to look at him to know that his jaw is cut from stone and his eyes are narrowed like a wolf about to rip the throat out of his prey.

From the corner of my eye, I see his hand grip his gun. "Tommy, why the fuck you bringing clowns into my home who can't follow basic instructions?" His voice grits through his clenched teeth.

"Listen, Knox, I don't mean no disrespect, man," Jim holds up his palms. "I can do ten though. You don't need to work me up slow. I'm good."

"What the fuck are you doing?" Tommy hisses at him. Jim doesn't respond. His eyes are locked on Knox.

"You'll take four, or you'll take none. You have one fucking week to get me my cut, five grand. You make the math work, but don't cut it with too much shit or you won't get any repeat business, got it?"

"How about I start with six?" Jim answers coolly.

"This isn't a fucking negotiation!" Knox thunders.

Jim clamps his mouth shut, but he doesn't shirk back. My eyes travel over his ropy muscles, dipping down to the bulge of his pants. He's packing, and I know from Knox's pat down routine, that it ain't a gun. I don't mean to squeeze my thighs tight. I don't give my pussy permission to get wet. I've just never seen someone challenge Knox so nonchalantly. There's something about his quiet confidence that's hard not to admire.

"Fine, man. Four it is. You're the boss," Jim agrees. His tone is flat though. His ice blue eyes flicker between my legs and he quickly licks his lip before returning his focus to the job. It was a second, less than that, but it was enough to make my nipples turn to pebbles. Who is this guy?

"Take yer shit and get out." Knox nods to the brick. "You've got one week. Don't make me send someone collecting."

"I won't." Jim quickly snatches the block of blow from the table and thrusts it into his jacket pocket.

We all stand up. The men don't shake hands. Instead Knox and Jim stare at each other like a couple of dogs ready to fight.

"Let's go, man," Tommy nods toward the door.

Jim doesn't move. Tommy grabs him by his elbow and leads him away. As Tommy turns the knob on the door, Jim turns and looks back at us.

"I'll see you in a week." His eyes are clearly locked on me.

"Bye." I'm not sure why the word escaped my lips. Let alone why it came out all high-pitched and singsongy.

The men disappear through the door and Knox quickly walks over to it, locking it behind them.

I start to make my way to the bathroom when Knox marches up to me.

"You fucking little slut!" Bright white light jolts over my eyes as he throws me into the wall.

His hand squeezes around my throat, locking me in place and cutting off my air.

"You think you're here to flirt with my guys, bitch?" The back of his hand slices across my lip and I can instantly taste my blood.

"Knox," I sputter, "please."

His fist is wrapped in my long brown hair and he tosses me to the floor. I hit it with a thud.

"That's right, Holly. You'll be begging me all night." He unbuckles his belt and quickly flicks the leather free, snapping it toward me like a whip. "You'll beg me to stop. Then you'll beg me to fuck you."

Eddie Cleveland

CHAPTER 2
Holly

With a quick jerk of his wrist, Knox snaps the leather belt across my bare leg. The pain spreads over my flesh like wildfire. My eyes water, but I don't cry out. I've learned he likes that more. I won't give him the fucking satisfaction.

Knox sneers down at me. His brown eyes flicker with a rage I've seen more times than I'd like to admit.

SNAP!

Tears spill onto my cheeks as welts begin to rise on my calf. I desperately try to get my feet under me. I push myself up, attempting to stand.

"Where do you think you're going?" Knox's foot lands square on my stomach. I collapse back onto the floor, gasping for air. He knocked the wind out of me.

"I'm not even close to being finished with you, Holly."

Knox wraps the belt tightly around his tattooed fist, his shoulders hunch over as he towers me. The silver buckle of his belt dangles menacingly before me, promising pain to come.

"Knox, please… "

SNAP!

The buckle hits my arm like a rock.

"No! Please! I'm sorry, ok? I'm sorry!" I choke out the words, tears flooding my face. I hate myself for begging him. I hate myself for ever staying with him. I hate… him.

Knox stands taller, proud that he broke me down. I frantically look to the lone exit from his condo. It's behind him. The only other escape is the balcony. I'd never survive. Eighteen floors up would kill me.

Wouldn't that be better?

I push the thought away. No. I won't let him kill me. I won't go down without a fight. Not anymore.

Knox lifts his arm again; I scuttle back on the floor. I won't lie here and let him beat me. I need to try.

His belt buckle comes down, but doesn't bite my skin. I scurry backward as I see the fire in his eyes blaze out of control.

"Fucking cunt! Where do you think you're gonna go, huh? You want me to chase you around the room?" He snarls.

"Knox, please. Put down the belt," I plead.

"After what you did? I brought you into my home and took care of you, for how long? Years! Treated you like a little princess and you sit on my lap with your pussy leaking for some other guy?" He leaps toward me, the belt buckle glistening under the light.

"I didn't!" I protest, shifting backward as quickly as I can manage.

SNAP!

"Fuck!" The buckle meets my ankle and blinding pain sears through me. I don't have time to hold it. To check it. To see if it's broken. I need to get away.

I move back and thump into the coffee table. Quickly, I cower under it, then tip it over, trying to barricade myself from Knox's abuse. The table hits the floor with a thud. My mind reels for a better plan. I silently pray for help when the cool metal slides against my hand.

His gun.

The gun I've never seen him without, a single day. The one that's always out. Always loaded. The silencer, always screwed on tight. It just slid from the table to the floor beside my hand.

I blink, uncertain of how the gun ended up in my hand. I don't remember picking it up. I don't remember aiming it at him. My brain is in survival mode.

Knox is perfectly still. The smug smile on his face tells me just how serious he thinks this is. He hasn't even dropped the belt.

"Oh, come on," he smiles. He's clearly amused. "You gonna shoot me?" He takes a slow, deliberate step forward.

"Stay back!" Hot tears blur my vision. I raise the gun to his head and cock it. It's heavier than I imagined.

Knox's smile fades. "You won't," his voice is confident but he doesn't move. "You need me, Holly. We need each other."

My hand trembles. If I drop this gun, I know how this

ends. My body covered in welts as he roughly fucks me. I know that tomorrow, he'll buy me expensive clothes, and that we'll never talk about this. About what he does to me. Until next time. When it happens again.

And again.

"No!" My voice is steadier than my hand. "I don't need you anymore."

"If you shoot me, you better fucking kill me, cunt! I'll fuck you with that gun, you understand me?" Knox booms.

I drop my hand, and Knox sneers as he thinks that he won. Instead, I aim between his legs, I'm going to shoot his dick off. The trigger squeezes easily under my finger. I close my eyes and lower the gun.

BANG!

"Fucking-shit-fuck! You bitch!"

I open my eyes and Knox is on the floor holding his knee. Not what I was aiming for, but satisfaction still swells up inside me as I watch the blood stain his jeans.

There's no time to waste! I spot his car keys on the bookshelf and run across the room to grab them.

"I'm gonna slice you open! Do you hear me?" Knox shrieks.

Clutching the keys in my free hand, I grip his gun tight in my other. I hold it up again, pointing it at him as I maneuver around his bloody pool growing on the floor.

"Fuck you, Knox." I grit the words through my teeth. "If you ever come near me again, I'll kill you with your own fucking gun," I yell bravely.

I run to the door and don't look back as I pass through

it. I know he can't chase me down, but somehow I'm not convinced he won't find a way. I race down the stairwell so fast I feel like I'm almost tumbling down the flights of stairs. My ankle is screaming in pain, but I can't stop. I can't risk him catching me. Not now.

Knox will kill me. Or have someone else do it. The fluorescent lights blend together as I race through the underground parking lot to his car. Jumping in, I half expect him to hit the window, like some kind of goddamned horror movie villain that won't die. He's been far worse than that for me, for a long time now.

The key turns in the ignition and the car starts. I back out and Knox isn't there. I make it all the way to the exit, expecting this to somehow fall apart at any second. I shiver despite the Miami heat.

Nothing stops me. I pull out onto the street and drive away into the night. All my fears of never being able to escape slowly begin to fade as I realize what I just did. I've been with Knox so long; I had convinced myself freedom was impossible. I toss his handgun into the passenger seat and drive away. Knox and his horrors grow smaller in my rearview mirror as my mind fumbles to come up with a plan. I'll need to ditch the car. I need to get out of Florida. But where will I go? How will I get there?

I only know two things right now.

I'm free.

If Knox tracks me down, I'll be dead.

Eddie Cleveland

CHAPTER 3

Jake

"Petty Officer Armstrong!" My head snaps up and my eyes refocus to the present. Back from the hundred-mile stare – the look I get when the past haunts my memories.

"Chief!" I answer Chief Warrant Officer Andrews, who's been assigned to represent me at my hearing.

My Captain's Mast is a blessing compared to the court-martial I could've been up for. However, just because it's a lesser punishment doesn't mean I'm not about to get tossed out of the SEALs. I know I'm not going to spend any time in a cell, but I might be given my marching orders. Back to civilian street.

"You come to attention when I address you, Petty Officer! This is a charge parade not a fucking tea party," Andrews barks, his cheeks billowing out like a sail in high seas.

"Yes, Chief!" I stand at attention. Eyes forward. Chin

up. Shoulders back. I refuse to let my gaze wander over to the man now responsible for representing me. A man I've served with for years. Closer to me than my own father. My gut twinges as the thought marinates in my brain. Just like my own Dad, he's a man I've let down.

"Now, listen here," the Chief continues, "you're gonna march down these flats and before you enter the quarterdeck you're gonna remove your headdress, got it?" He doesn't wait for my response. It wasn't a real question.

My eyes flicker over his aging face. He meets my gaze with a hardened stare, his brown eyes leveling me. "You're gonna march over to the podium and bring your heels together in front of the Captain. You don't say a word. Not a fucking peep. You let me do the talking, understand?" He paces in front of me nervously.

Again, I don't answer, but this time I can see that Andrews wanted me to. He stops and peers at me with a look that makes me wish I could hide in my own skin. How is it that I can face terrorists? I can shoot killers dead without a second thought, but a look from Andrews makes me feel like a nervous recruit again.

"Yes, Chief!" I answer.

Andrews nods slowly, happy with my delayed response. His sea boots squeak against the floor as he goes back to pacing.

"Good. Now, the Captain will hear your charges. He'll listen to what I have to say and then he'll ask you to speak. A word of advice, keep it short, sweet and true. No excuses. No one wants to hear anything other than your total acceptance that what you did was wrong, get it?"

"Yes, Chief!"

"I'm gonna recommend that we keep you, Armstrong. I'll do what I can. However, there's a good chance you're being discharged. If that happens," he stops in his tracks and looks me square in the face, "I want to thank you."

I can't hide the surprise spreading over my face like an oil slick on the ocean. My jaw slackens, "Thank me?"

"Yes," the Chief's face is inches from my own. I can see the broken capillaries in his nose that tell the tale of more fun nights out with the boys than he probably remembers. The smell of his tobacco chew wafts around me. "Listen, son, I know you. I've known you for many years now. I know as well as anybody that this was a mistake. An idiotic mistake, but it wasn't you. You're more than your worst decision. There isn't a single person on this earth that wants to be judged on their lowest moment. Trust me, we've all done shit we aren't proud of," he claps my shoulder and his eyes soften.

I look down at the toes of my boots, wishing with every ounce of my soul that I could take it all back. But I can't.

"If you do get the boot today, it doesn't change what you did for us, for your brothers, or for your country over in Afghanistan. You carried out that mission and saved lives. This…" he waves his hand searching for the word, "shit show that you've gotten yourself into, it's never gonna taint that. So, thank you. Keep your chin up and be proud of what you did right. Even if your life feels all wrong now. You'll always have that."

Andrews clears his throat loudly and squares off his jaw. As he clamps his teeth together, his eyes narrow and the moment between us fades away.

"Now, march your ass down to the quarterdeck. Let's get this over with," he barks.

"Yes, Chief!" I repeat again as I give an about-turn and do my sharpest drill down the hall.

As I was directed, I stop and remove my hat before proceeding into the room. My arms swing by my sides as I take short, sharp steps over to the podium. I come to a standstill in front of the Captain, snap my heels together and stiffly hold my arms tight to my sides.

Captain Bliss looks me over sternly. His thick moustache seems to add an extra layer of disapproval with its turned down sides. The look of disgust is echoed in his squinted eyes and furrowed brows.

I struggle to focus as Andrews pleads my case. My mind is reeling, is this it for me? I joined the SEALs just days after I graduated high school. This career is one I've lived and breathed for my entire adult life. If I'm not a SEAL, who will I be?

"I said, 'what do you have to say for yourself, Armstrong?'" The Captain's voice reaches through the thick cotton fog in my brain and gives me a shake.

I blink as I realize everyone is waiting for me to say my piece. Swallowing hard, I open my mouth, "Sir. Sorry, Sir. I'm guilty. The cocaine was mine and I used it for recreational purposes. I have no excuse. It was a bad decision, Sir. One I've regretted every day since. I let down my brothers in arms and I also let down my real brother, in an act of cowardice I'll never be able to forgive myself for. I accept your judgement and punishment."

"Captain, if I may," Andrews cuts in, "I'd like to say a few words," he waits for the nod of approval from Bliss before continuing.

"Very well," the Captain answers.

Andrews clears his throat, "Sir, I'd like to add that Petty

Officer Armstrong has worked with me for quite some time. He's always been reliable and respectful; a stand-up guy. He's served us proudly abroad on many deployments as well as at home. I see you have his file there," Andrews nods to the manila envelope on the podium, "so I don't need to tell you how instrumental Armstrong was in Operation Trident Fury. However, I would just like to mention that without the unflinching bravery that this man showed during that mission, our guys could have easily faced an ambush." My Chief looks over at me, "He definitely stepped in it this time. I'm not saying he should be excused for what he did, I just want to let you know that what he did was a mistake and not at all a testament to his character."

Captain Bliss looks at me sternly, then to the Chief. "Noted," he finally answers.

The room is so quiet. Every movement of the people gathered to watch this humiliating proceeding is amplified like its being played over a loudspeaker. I can hear Andrews breathing beside me. I can hear my own heart rushing blood through my body.

"The charges against you are serious, Petty Officer," the Captain finally interrupts the silence. "Cocaine use is strictly prohibited, as you well know. However, given your clean record, not to mention your exemplary reputation that Chief Warrant Officer Andrews just mentioned about your deployment with SEAL Team 8, you went above and beyond for your mission and I'm prepared to take that into consideration." He presses his lips into little more than a slit in his face, his moustache covering his mouth like a blanket. "Your punishment," he looks at me sternly, "you will receive a full reduction in rank, a loss of fifty percent of your base pay for two months and you must also attend an inpatient rehabilitation facility for sixty days. If you choose not to attend, which you are within your legal rights to refuse, you will be discharged. What do you choose?" He watches me carefully.

Is it really a choice? The money and rank reduction sting, but both can be earned back. Getting a discharge would be death.

"I accept your first option. Thank you, Sir."

CHAPTER 4

Holly

ERREICH!
"Fuck!" I yank the wheel hard to the right and pull back down off the curb I'd just driven Knox's car onto. That didn't sound good, but I don't have time to care. I grab the ticket from the airport parking garage dispenser and shakily maneuver his precious Audi inside.

Somehow, I manage to slide into an open parking space without crashing the car into anything else. When I ran away from home at seventeen, all I had was a learner's permit. I've been behind the wheel before, but that was five years ago. I throw the car into park and fling my seatbelt off, patting my hands underneath the dashboard carefully.

"I know it's here somewhere," I grunt, twisting my body into some kind of advanced yoga pose as I reach as far as my fingertips can stretch.

"There!" I feel the bundle and pry the duct tape by

the corner, peeling it back until the package fall into my hand. Yanking the Ziploc bag of money toward me, I quickly dart my eyes out my window to see if anyone around is watching. The few people in the parking garage are busy getting their bags together for their trips. No one gives a damn about what I'm doing, let alone what I'm going through.

I pull the bag open and wrap my trembling hand around the stack of bills inside. The wad of neatly wrapped hundred dollar bills is mine. I've been with Knox for five years, and for as long as I've known him, he's kept his emergency stash of cash taped up in his car. He always said it was enough to get to where he had to go if shit went down, but not so much that it would ruin him if his car ever got jacked. Knox isn't big on bank accounts. Instead, he has bricks of cash like this one hidden all over the condo and lord knows where else.

I flip my thumb over the bills, there's at least ten grand here. I can go anywhere with that kind of cash. Anywhere in the world. Start over. Go get a fresh start somewhere.

Like the fresh start you got with Knox?

I wave my hand, trying to swat the intrusive thought away like a buzzing mosquito. This will be different. I'm not a kid anymore. I won't end up in the arms of another psychopathic drug smuggler. I've always learned my lessons the hard way, but I still learn them.

I don't have my purse, so I split the fat wad of cash in two and stuff each half into the cups of my bra. I look like Dolly Parton, but I don't care. I'd probably get a lot more stares if I walked around holding ten thousand dollars in my hand like a clutch. My eyes flit over the car to see if there's anything else I should bring. They stop on the gun lying on the passenger seat, gleaming up at me. I spin around in my seat and cautiously look around for any security guards or passersby who might notice what I'm doing. No one around. Quickly, I wrap my fingers around the cold steel and give the gun a quick wipe down using the stretchy edge of my skirt to lift it back up and toss it under the driver's seat. I pull the keys from the ignition and cast them aside the same way. One quick look in the mirror to make sure I don't have raccoon eyes, and I'm out of Knox's car. I lock the door, slam it shut and gasp instinctively at the gash slit down the driver's side door from where I scraped the ticket box.

Knox would kill me if he saw that. Shit, Knox will kill me if he ever sees me again. The car should be the least of my worries. After half a decade of living with his rules, his anger, his abuse…it's hard to shake the feeling that everything I'm doing won't come with horrifying consequences.

I need to get away. Start over. I need to go now. Logically, I know that with a gunshot wound to the leg, Knox isn't going to be hot on my tail chasing me down. It's not like he can just call in his car stolen to the Miami police. They would love to hear from him, as one of the biggest cocaine importers on the Eastern Seaboard, I'm sure it would be the bust of a lifetime for them, to have Knox drop into their laps.

No, I don't need to worry about any of that. For now. I slam the door shut and make my way to the airport. I just need to get on a flight and get out of here. The further the better. My heels click against the cement loudly as I struggle to think up a plan. Maybe Europe would be a good place to go.

Shit.

I can't leave the country! Not when I left my passport at my parents' house five years ago. My mind flashes back to a similar time, when I let my parents think I was going off to school, my backpack stuffed with my belongings. Instead of heading to my grade eleven classes that day, I jumped on a bus for Miami. After grieving my twin sister's death for almost a year, I couldn't take it anymore. I could deal with the stares, the whispers, the rumors. I couldn't, however, handle the emotionless void in my mother's eyes, or the heartbroken and forced smiles from my Dad. I had to leave it behind. To start over. I left and never looked back.

After living in a town as small as Everglades City, getting lost in a real city like Miami seemed perfect. It didn't take me too many nights on my own before I realized how wrong I'd been. A fresh-faced seventeen-year-old in a huge city, it wasn't long before I attracted the wrong kind of attention.

I saved you, you ungrateful cunt! Without me, you'd be turning tricks on the street. Or dead.

Knox's words that I've heard so many times echo in my mind. My heart wrenches as hot tears slide down my cheeks. I remember when being his girl felt like a privilege. When he really did feel like my knight in shining armor. I was so young and fucking dumb.

I wipe away the tears with the back of my hand, the welts on my leg and my swollen ankle are painful reminders of how wrong I was. A salty tear trails down my face and burns the split in my lip, making me wince.

No, I don't owe him shit. He didn't save me. He ruined me.

I reach the door of the airport and my stomach sinks. I

have no ID at all. None. It's not just a matter of having no passport. I didn't have the time or the presence of mind to grab my purse when I ran out of Knox's place. I'm not just stuck in the USA, I'm stuck. Period.

I fight the urge to lay down and give up. To just crumple into a fetal position and let the authorities deal with me. I'm exhausted. The adrenaline of leaving Knox behind has faded out and, for the first time in five years, so has my coke high.

When I first came to live with Knox, I remember how the endless partying and mountains of coke would light up our nights. What started as fun quickly turned into necessity. I began using coke how most people drink coffee. After a while, I needed it just to feel normal. I haven't been clean in almost half a decade. Right now, I'm fading fast.

Without thinking, I jump into one of the yellow cabs waiting by the airport curb. I feel cocooned inside the car. Safer than I've felt in years.

The cab driver turns to me, the white teeth revealed in his smile are a stark contrast to his midnight skin. "Where can I take you?" He asks cheerfully in a thick Jamaican accent.

Where? Where can I go?

Tears blur my vision and flood my face. "I… I don't know," I sob.

"Whoa, hey now. Don't cry. It'll be ok," worry flashes over his dark features as his eyes flicker over my swollen lip. "Are you in danger? I can call the police if you want?" His velvety voice wraps around me like a soothing hug.

"No!" I yelp. "Please, no police," I wave my hand frantically.

"Ok, ok," he answers. "Don't worry. We'll figure it out together. Do you have any friends you can go to?"

I solemnly shake my head from side to side as tears choke off my words.

"Ok, how about family. Surely you have a mother and father? Right?" He prods.

"I can't see them. I haven't talked to them in five years. I don't think they ever want to see me again anyway," I whimper.

"Hold up. Listen to me young lady," his thick Jamaican accent rolls his words, "I am a father of three girls," he holds up his fingers at me to clarify. "I wouldn't care if I hadn't heard from them in fifty years, if they called me, I'd take that call. You don't know a parent's love for a child. You can trust that." His kind eyes are comforting.

"I don't have a way to call them," I explain. "I have money for this trip, but I didn't take anything else when I ran… I mean, when I left." I try to keep the details to myself.

The cab driver nods slowly, digesting my words. "Listen, young lady, that's no problem. You can call your folks on my phone. No charge. Just call them. I promise you, they'll want to help you."

He hands his cellphone back to me and I stare at it blankly. It's been so long since I left. Since I walked away from the confusion, hurt and despair I caused them. Will they be happy to hear from me? After what I did? After this much time?

"Please, as a father, I beg you. Call them." He repeats.

Breathing in deeply, I dial the number I grew up with.

A number I haven't pressed into any phone for years. My shaking hand holds the cell to my ear as a broad smile flashes over the cab driver's face.

Br-ring! Br-ring!

"Hello?" My father's voice cuts through the years of silence. I can't speak. I can picture him so clearly, as his voice tethers me to reality. "Hello?" He repeats.

"Daddy," my voice cracks as my tears flow freely now.

"Holly? Oh my God! Holly, is that you?" His voice is strained with desperation.

"Yes. Dad? I need help."

CHAPTER 5

Holly

The yellow cab lazily lumbers into my parents' driveway like we're traveling underwater. Time comes to a standstill as I manage to separate four sweaty hundred dollar bills from my bra and hand them over.

"This is too much," the driver gently corrects me.

"I owe you much more than that," I answer. The hour and a half drive might have come to just over two hundred, but I am more than grateful for the kindness this stranger has shown me. Besides, I have no problem spending cash from a man who earned it keeping people like me addicted to drugs.

"Thank you," his teeth flash a brilliant white as he smiles.

I open the door and step out onto wobbly legs. My knees threaten to buckle beneath me, like a newborn fawn standing for the first time. Exhaustion battles with my nervousness, making my head spin with the terrible concoction.

I slam the door to the cab shut behind me and pull a deep breath of fresh air into my lungs. This is it. I haven't seen my parents in five years. I don't know what to expect. I don't know what to say. I don't...

"Holly!" My father explodes from the front door in his tattered, brown slippers and his robe flapping behind his flannel pajamas like the superman cape I used to imagine he secretly wore under his clothes when I was a child.

Suddenly, the world speeds up as Dad runs down the front steps and over to me. It's a blur as he throws his arms around me, tears cascading down my face as I tuck my head into my father's chest.

"Daddy," I croak the word. My emotions are a cyclone of confusion. In a way, it feels like it was only yesterday that I left without looking back. In many more ways, it feels like it was a lifetime ago.

My father grabs my shoulders and locks his brown eyes on mine. "Where did you go? Why did you leave? Are you ok? What happened to your mouth? Oh my God, I'm so happy to see you!" He rattles off his questions in rapid fire. "You know what? It doesn't matter. You're home now. That's the main thing," he folds me into him, holding me in another tight bearhug. "Let's get you inside," he steps back.

I follow his lead toward the house and watch as the cab driver pulls back out of the driveway and onto the suburban street. The darkness obscures my view of him, but he changes gears under the streetlight and I can see the sweet smile spread across his face as he drives away.

I step inside my parents' house and nothing has changed. The living room furniture with the worn navy blue stripes is in the same place as when I left. On the wall are the same photos, encapsulating our family in a moment we probably all wish we could go back to. A moment where we looked genuinely happy. A moment when Heather, my twin, was still alive.

The only thing that has changed is that I don't see my mother anywhere. I scan the room, but she's nowhere to be seen. Her shoes are still in the front hall and her knitting is sitting half-finished on the coffee table. I know she's still living here.

"Where's Mom?" I turn my face toward my father. His deep wrinkles burrow into his skin as he frowns. "She's here, honey. She went to bed. She just needs time, ok?" He explains so softly, his voice is like a summer breeze. Yet the words smack me in the face as hard as the back of Knox's hand.

She doesn't want me here. She doesn't want to see me. I never should've come home.

"Here, you can wear this," Dad slides his tattered robe off his arms and onto my shoulders. I remember that Heather and I gave him this housecoat for Father's Day when we were nine. I can't believe he's hung onto it for thirteen years. I slip my arms inside and glance up at my father's face. His eyes are clouded with tears as he gazes down over my skin-tight, short dress.

Shame floods me as I pull on the robe and wrap myself in it, like a protective blanket, trying to hide what only hours ago felt like perfectly acceptable clothes. I can see the disappointment in my father's face as he tries to piece together my disappearance. As he tries to make sense of all of this.

"Holly, are you in trouble? Do you… are you…? Well,

are you running from someone? A pimp?" His voice trembles.

A pimp?

I don't know what to say. Is the truth any better? I may not have been working the streets, but Knox always took everything from me when he wanted it. It didn't start out that way. It never used to be shelter and coke in exchange for sex. At least, that's what I told myself when he first took me in. Of course, to a seventeen-year-old runaway, a twenty-seven-year-old with money and power was alluring. Add the idea of him loving me to the mix and I never had a chance.

"No, I'm not a prostitute. I swear." The relief washing over my father's aging face breaks my heart.

"What happened to you? Where did you go?" He leads me over to the couch and I curl my feet up under me as I sit down on it. The warmth of the house, his housecoat, knowing for the first time in almost half a decade that I'm safe, it's all making my eyelids heavy.

"I ended up in Miami," I confess, my voice thick with exhaustion. "I ended up with a man. A really bad man. Dad?" I somehow manage to pry my eyes open to look up at my father. His nose looks bigger than the last time I saw him. His ears too. My eyes start to travel over his face, lined deep with worry. Aged beyond his years. He's lost most of his hair, too. The thin, salt and pepper clinging to the sides of his head and combed over his shiny bald spot is fooling no one.

"Are you in danger now? What can I do to help you?" Dad prods.

"I am, Dad, he is a drug smuggler. One of the biggest on the East Coast. If he finds me, he's gonna kill me. I swear, he's terrible. I need to get clean and I need to get help. I want to start over. I want to get off the drugs and start a new life. He doesn't know where I am, I never told him where I came from. Plus, I parked his car at an airport to make him think I flew somewhere. He won't look for me here. But, I still can't stay here. Daddy," fat tears stream down my face and drip off my chin, blotting on his robe, "I need to get real help. For drugs. I need to get clean." I repeat and I see the realization of what I'm telling him takes hold of my father's face.

Five years ago, if I would've admitted to using cocaine, hell, even pot, my Dad probably would've kicked me out to the very streets I ran away to. Now, I can see the years have softened him. I suppose losing not only one, but both of your children will do that. Guilt floods through me, coursing through my veins as I realize for the first time the pain and suffering I've put him through. I've put them both through.

"Ok, we'll get you into rehab. There's plenty of good programs out there, we'll do some research and find the right one." Dad nods and throws his shoulders back with determination.

"I can help pay. I have money," I reach inside the robe and pull the wads of bills out, lying them on the couch between us.

"Where the hell did you get all of this?" Dad's eyes flash with suspicion, no doubt questioning if I have been working the streets after all.

"I took it from him. He was beating me, Dad. He… he hurt me all the time. I couldn't take it anymore so I left." I start explaining.

Dad holds up his hands and I fall silent. "Ok, enough.

It's late, it's been a crazy day. I'm sure you're tired."

I nod.

"So am I," his voice grows weary as his face falls. "Tomorrow, we'll figure this all out. We'll get you into rehab. We'll make a plan. For tonight, I think the best thing any of us can do is get a good night's sleep. Ok?" His tone tells me he isn't really asking, he's telling me. That's fine with me.

"Sure." I mumble.

"Your room is still how you left it, Holly. You can sleep in there." He instructs me.

I stand up and shuffle over to the stairs. I try not to limp on my bad ankle. I don't want to worry my father any more than I already have. As I approach the stairs, I hear my mother scurry from the top back to her room and shut the door.

She was listening the whole time.

I make my way to my room. Dad was right; it hasn't changed a bit. The bedding looks fresh on the single sized bed, but other than that it looks like a time capsule in here. My collection of cheap perfumes is still lined up on my dresser and my poster of Channing Tatum is still tacked to the wall. I slump into my bed and yank the covers over me, still fully dressed. Sleep quickly begins to overtake me as I relax back against my pillow.

My mother's voice makes me startle. I can hear her getting louder as my father tries to hush her. Is she yelling? I tilt my head toward my bedroom door and listen. No, she's crying. My heart sinks.

"It won't change anything," she sobs. "You can send her to rehab, you can do everything you can, but it won't change a damned thing!" Her voice is shrill.

She's never forgiven me. She still hates me. Blames me as much as she did six years ago, when it happened.

The day my sister died.

CHAPTER 6

Jake

April 1st. What a day to be sent off to rehab. I guess that makes me the April fool. More like fuck-up. I watch the massive cedars slide by the window of the taxi. On the other side of the highway, the Pacific Ocean quietly laps at the shoreline. I'm not sure why the brass decided to send me to British Columbia, Canada, of all places. The United States probably has more top-notch rehabilitation centers than any other country on earth.

I watch the calm, green waves of the Pacific, mesmerized. I've lived and sailed on the Atlantic my entire career. I've grown to love her wild, uncontrollable swells and her craggy shorelines. The Pacific seems more refined, her gentle rolls hypnotically grazing the sandy beach. They're like twin sisters, separated at birth. One reckless and free, the other reserved and shy.

I might not be drawn to the water in the same way, but it's hard to argue that there's a tranquility in this landscape that soothes the soul. The softly sloping mountains in the distance, the giant evergreens stretching toward the overcast sky. I feel like I'm driving through a Bob Ross painting. Now we just need to turn my mistakes into 'happy little accidents' and I'll be all set.

The driver pulls into the long, curved driveway and up to the front door. I hand him the fare in American and he smiles brightly.

"You want me to figure out the exchange on that?" He nods his sallow face down to the bills in his hand.

"Nah, I'm good. Thanks, man." I pop open the door and hop out, glancing up at the sprawling brown building with the green roof in front of me.

It looks like the architect took his cue from the nature surrounding the building and made the facility the same color as the trees it's nestled in. I grab my bags from the trunk and slowly walk toward the front doors.

What am I doing here? I don't belong here. I'm not some crackhead or junkie. I just did coke to feel better. To stop the slow motion replay of that night. It helps me forget.

I give my head a shake and throw my shoulders back. I'm here because this is the only way I get to stay with the SEALs. It's just like every other training they've sent me on or tested me with. I just need to play the game, get through it and move on.

I pause at the door, my eye caught by the shiny black plaque on the wall. 'For Those Alumni who have lost their lives to chemical dependency' it reads. There must be at least a hundred names on there, and room for more. Not exactly a strong testament to the program I'm about to enter.

I sigh and push open the door. Let's get this over with.

The reception area has a pint-sized smiling woman greeting me as soon as I pass the threshold.

"Hello! Welcome to Edgewood. Are you a new patient?" Her grey eyes dart down to my bags.

"Yeah, I'm Petty Officer Armstrong. I was told you'd be expecting me to check in today."

"Certainly!" Her words are too cheerful. Her smile looks painful. I can't look at her, it makes me uncomfortable. "If you could just take a seat here and fill out these forms, I'll have a counselor come out to get you checked in."

Checked in. Like I'm taking a vacation at an all-inclusive. I grab the forms and scan the room as I make my way to the expensive looking leather chairs lining the wall. The place does look like a resort or some kind of spa. The floor-to-ceiling windows allow me to get a glimpse of the facility past this reception area. Cathedral glass ceilings and beautiful red cedar wood lumber draw my attention. Maybe this won't be so bad after all. I wonder if they have a pool.

I take a seat and fill out the information. I don't notice the short, slim man with a crooked smile who quietly sits in the chair next to me until he clears his throat and I look up.

"Hi, I'm John. I'll help you get settled in here, and show you around." His eyes blink quickly, like he has a tic he can't control.

"Uh, great. Sounds good," I stand up and hand off the paperwork to the woman with the pasted on smile. My fingers wrap around the handle of my suitcase when John holds up his hand.

"No, just leave those."

"What? I need them," I frown.

"They'll be delivered to your room, after they've been searched." He answers quietly but firmly.

"Searched. Seriously?"

"It's mandatory."

Another sigh escapes my lips and I let go of the handle with a shrug. "Fine. Whatever."

John swipes his ID card and the inside door clicks loudly as it unlocks for us. He opens it and holds it for me, his hand extended as an invite for me to pass through. Damned Canadians and their manners. It feels awkward to have a little man hold the door for me like we're on a date, but I push the feeling aside and enter.

John shuffles up next to me, showing different parts of the common areas. "Over there is the dining hall," he points vaguely toward the vacant cafeteria. "That is the nurses' station and medication dispensary. It's where you pick up your meds in the morning, if you need them," he nods to the sprawling wood desk ahead of us.

"I won't need any," I try to answer politely, but the words come out with a razor's edge.

I look around, where is everyone?

As if reading my thoughts, John answers my unasked question, "The other patients and counselors are in the auditorium for the morning lesson."

Lesson? Ok then. I don't bother asking what that's about. I'm sure in two months, I'll be getting more than my fill of the routine here.

All of a sudden, the eerie silence crashes around us as a huge group of people come from the hallways on either side of the desk and flood into the space. Their combined voices sound like a flock of angry seagulls fighting for scraps of food at the beach. People are mulling around with binders in their arms, like they're in school.

I'm surprised how many of them look normal. I mean, I guess I expected people to be more disheveled and have less teeth, generally. John is saying something, but I can't hear him. I can't even hear the grating caws of the bustling crowd anymore. My feet stop moving and my eyes lock down.

She's striking. Not like some photoshopped super model, perfectly made up with smoky eyes and red lips. She's a natural beauty. I'm transfixed by her plump lips. I'm hypnotized by her perky breasts and the curve of her ass. It's easy to see from the sparkle in her baby blue eyes that she has a wild streak I'd love to explore. In a way, she reminds me of the Atlantic Ocean I was missing before. Untamed and mysterious. I want to wrap my hands in her long, wavy brown hair. I want to kiss every inch of her milky skin. Her eyes quickly find mine and I can see she feels it too. My heart pounds as I try to stop staring.

I can't.

I watch as the cute freckles on her pale skin crinkle up and her eyebrows knit together. She looks away from me, toward the tall, built man that is standing too close to her and talking too loudly. My fists clench and my teeth set on edge as I watch her pull her binder up over her perfect tits, like a shield. A move I've seen tons of women do, and never when they're comfortable with the guy bothering them. She steps back from the obnoxious dude towering over her and he lumbers forward, refilling the empty space. Anger flashes through me and I step forward, just as John grabs my shoulder.

"Where are you going?" He tilts his head at me.

"Uh, I just need to use the toilet," I lie, hoping he buys it.

"Ahh, ok. Well, you can do that in a bit. First, you need to follow me," he insists.

I look back up, but the girl is gone. I don't see her anywhere in the crowd. She disappeared.

"Ok, what's up?" I follow John into one of the offices lining the wall. It's instantly quieter as he closes the door.

"As you probably know, Edgewood is a renowned facility. We have a program that specializes in addictions faced by men and women in uniform." He spouts off his talking points.

Ah, well that explains why I'm in Canada then.

"The program is difficult, but if you don't give up, we have an eighty percent success rate." He continues.

"That's pretty good," my mind flashes back to the plaque on the wall as I came in. Seems to contradict what he's telling me, but the truth is, I don't care. I can barely concentrate on what this guy is going on about. My mind is still wrapped up in her.

Where did she go?

"But before we get into any of that, we need to take the standard precautions to make sure you're not smuggling any drugs or paraphernalia into the facility," he continues.

"Yeah, well, you've already got my bags." I answer distractedly.

"Yes, that's part of it. However, there's another part. You're gonna need to strip down and shake out your clothes for me."

"What?" I level him with my stare, my focus suddenly sharpening to him and him alone. "Are you saying…"

"Before we can proceed, there's a strip search," he states matter-of-factly.

"Seriously?"

"Seriously," he answers.

So much for checking into my luxury spa. More like being processed for prison. This shit just got real.

Eddie Cleveland

CHAPTER 7
Holly

"Holly, you've been quiet for the past couple of days. I know you're still new to all of this, but why don't you tell the group about yourself?" My group therapy counselor, Gavin, prods me. He sits tall in his chair at one end of the circle, his hair gelled into a spiky hedgehog style that was popular when I was in junior high. His mournful brown eyes pierce mine.

"Uh, sure, I guess," I stare at my hands. I can't bring myself to look into the faces of the strangers surrounding me. Six people from all walks of life sit around me. Since I checked in two days ago, I've heard them talk about their lives, their careers, their children, their dreams. Intensely personal details have spilled out of them, like they've known these people all their lives. Like we've all grown up together. Not like we're the complete and total random strangers tossed together in a salad of sadness and sickness.

I clear my throat as my mind goes blank. What does he

want me to say?

"Do you mean tell you how I got started with drugs?" I peer over at Gavin and his thin sweeping of chin whiskers quiver as he presses his lips together.

"No, we'll get into all that. Right now, I would just like it if you introduced yourself to the group. Tell us who you are. A little bit about yourself," Gavin's eyes are warm, even if his tone is a bit clinical. He looks down at the pad of paper he's holding on a clipboard in his lap and makes a few notes.

A bit about myself? What is there to tell? A whirlwind of memories flash through my mind, but every single one of them involves Knox and cocaine. I squeeze my eyes shut, trying to concentrate on the question. It shouldn't be this hard. I should be able to tell people something. Anything.

Heat flushes over my cheeks as I blush, I open my eyes and try not to let the shame radiating through me turn to tears. "I don't know," I whisper. "I don't know who I am."

Gavin nods sadly and makes another note. The door to the office swings open and, lucky for me, all eyes in the room turn to see why. I watch as the guy I saw earlier today saunters inside and nonchalantly slumps down in an empty seat across the circle from me.

My heartbeat quickens as his deep blue eyes meet mine. He locks me in his gaze, and I feel like I'm struggling to keep my feet under me in a hurricane. I can feel the electricity crackle in the air between us, holding me prisoner of his stare. I press my thighs together tightly and my breathing grows raspy and erratic. I've never had such a visceral reaction to a man before. Not even to Knox.

Gavin clears his throat, ignoring our newest group member entirely. The same way he did to me two days ago when I was thrown into this jumbled mess of addicts. "You were saying, Holly?" His voice cuts through the fog and pulls me back into the therapy session.

Somehow, I manage to drag my eyes from the newcomer and back to my counselor. "What? Oh, yeah. I guess I was trying to say that I'm not sure how to tell you a bit about myself because it's been awhile since I've been more than, well, you know… an addict." I admit.

I look back over to the new guy; he's watching me closely. I'm sure every person in this room is, but his are the only eyes I feel on me. Like they're marking my skin. His brown beard is well kept, but the same can't be said for his shaggy hair. I force myself to focus on Gavin instead. No matter how difficult it is.

"It's been a long time since I've done anything other than be a drug smuggler's girlfriend. For the last five years, my whole life has centered on coke," I continue. "Selling it, using it, buying it. Everything has been focused on drugs." I answer truthfully.

Gavin makes another note and scratches the side of his head with his pen. "Ok, but what about hobbies? Or friends? Family?" He grasps at straws as I shake my head no at each suggestion.

"I left my family when I was seventeen and never looked back. I didn't really have a good idea of who I was when I ran away, just who I didn't want to be seen as anymore." My voice creaks, warning me of tears to come. "I don't know, ok?" I push away the sadness with a burst of anger. "I don't know what you're looking for. I've told you who I am, can we move on now?" My eyes flicker back to the new guy. His pale pink lips are cocked into a half smile as he shamelessly scans his eyes over my body.

That look, that arrogance, it reminds me of…

Knox's face flashes before my eyes. The smirk that would possess his face when he'd wrap a belt around his hand, relishing what he was about to do to me.

I push the image from my head, but the anger inside me boils up. "What about him?" I point across the circle at the mystery man who joined us. "Why don't you get him to introduce himself instead of sitting there smiling like an idiot."

"Hey," Gavin's voice is so soft, it's almost a whisper, "I know you're new, but that's not how we do things. Besides, I'd appreciate it if you let me run my own group," he scolds me. "What you're doing is deflecting right now, Holly."

"Hey man, I don't mind," the gorgeous stranger sitting across from me finally speaks. My heart flutters at his deep voice.

"It's not necessary," Gavin holds up his hand. "We like to give new patients a few days to acclimate before they jump in. Today is Holly's day," he tries to redirect the focus.

"No, man, it's fine. Hi everyone, I'm Jake." He steamrolls over Gavin's attempts to take charge. "I was told not to give you my last name in here. That's kind of weird for me since I've been in the military since I was a teenager and I've been going by my last name only, since then." He chuckles and throws his arms over the back of his seat, leaning back comfortably. I'm happy that I don't have to fight the urge to watch him anymore. Since he's taken command of the room my eyes are just one of many sets on him.

Gavin writes furiously on his sheets as Jake continues, "Anyway, I'm just doing my time. I don't really need to be here, well not like you guys do," he nods at me and my cheeks burn. "I need to do a stint to keep my job, so if this is what I gotta do to stay with the SEALs then, so be it."

He's a SEAL? I glance at his shaggy hair and his beard again. The scruff perfectly lines his strong jaw and his sandy brown hair hangs around his face like a frame for his ocean blue eyes. He doesn't look military. His slightly amused look stokes the flames of my anger.

"Oh, you don't have to be here, huh?" I spit the words at him. I could smack his high and mighty look off his perfect face. "I guess the military sent you here for research then? Or just for fun?" My fists ball up at my sides.

"No, I'm here for coke." He says slowly, like he's a professor to an obtuse student. "Cocaine is addictive. If you do it enough you'll get addicted no matter what. That doesn't make you an addict, it makes the substance itself impossible to not get addicted to. It's not like you. I was just partying." His eyes never break from mine. I can't decide if I want them to or not.

"Oh wow, that's so cool how you're the only non-addict in a rehab center. It must feel great to be so high above all of us," I snap back. I know this isn't entirely fair. I don't really know this guy. He doesn't know me. After spending five years being told that I'm nothing, being told how much better Knox is and always will be than me, I can't take one more second of being looked down on. Especially not by some big, hot guy who thinks he's king shit.

"Excuse me," Gavin interrupts, clearly exasperated. "I already said that we'll get to you another day," he frowns at Jake. "This is Holly's time, so if you wouldn't mind…"

"I'm not saying that. I'm just saying we're different, that's all." Jake completely ignores our counselor, never taking his eyes off me. "I'm not like you. I spent my time fighting for our country with other guys and when we had downtime, we lived it up. That's it. I didn't come from some broken home or whatever. My parents loved me and all that shit." His words sucker punch me.

I struggle to breathe as I jump to my feet. I left my parents' house because I ruined their lives. My mother never forgave me for the day my sister died. Even when I left for this place, she couldn't look me in the eyes when she coldly said goodbye. I left her house when I was seventeen, but I haven't felt her love for a lot longer than that.

"Go fuck yourself, douche," I storm across the room and fling the office door open, slamming it behind me.

Hot tears splash down my cheeks as I stumble down the hallway. Fuck that guy. Fuck him with his arrogant smirk and his beautiful eyes. I try to douse the flames of desire he so quickly ignited in me. I'm so glad he's had a great life and a great family. That he's not broken and pathetic.

Like me.

CHAPTER 8

Jake

Standing in the front hallway, like a herd of cattle waiting for the gates to the field to be unlocked, I wait with the other patients. Apparently, after lunch we have a daily walk for an hour. What I find weird is that none of the counselors have bothered to let me know about the schedule. I wasn't given a pamphlet with timings on it. Instead, I've had to glean the information from other patients.

At lunch, I scanned the cafeteria for Holly, but I didn't see her. Instead, I was invited to sit at the table with some very chatty Canadians while we ate our choice of either lasagna or burritos and rice.

"Ya, buddy. It's a bit confusing around here at first," a ginger guy with the thickest glasses I've ever seen and a heavy, almost Boston sounding accent nattered away. "But you get used to it in no time. Once you learn the routine, it's like Groundhog Day in here." He scarfed his burrito and talked around the mushed beans as he chewed. "I've heard that you guys deal better with that though."

"You guys?" I looked up from my plate of meaty lasagna to question him.

"You military types. There's a lot of you in here. They say you're so used to doing routines and following orders that it's not too hard on you. Give it a day and you'll be a pro." He tossed the remaining burrito in his mouth and I looked around.

How many military people are there? I looked around the cafeteria wondering. With everyone dressed in civvies, it wasn't easy to see. Not until I started looking closer. Haircuts, posture, demeanor. They all helped me zone in on others who are serving their country.

Despite how intensely I looked through the crowd, there was one face I wanted to see that was missing. Holly.

The door buzzes and everyone shuffles through to the fresh air awaiting us outside. I smile up at the sun, breathing the clean West Coast air deep into my lungs. I stretch my arms in wide circles and shake out the tension. What a great day for a run.

I start to jog up the path leading through the thick cedars when a woman calls out behind me. I barely catch my name and stop.

Is it her?

My eyes focus like a red laser locking in on a target for the mystery person yelling my name. God damn. I would love to make her sweet lips call out my name. Cry it loudly as I make her cum over and over.

Disappointment crashes over me as my focus narrows

to a hunched over, silver-haired woman who could be my grandmother. "Jake," she smiles at me.

"Uh, yeah?" How does she know my name? Who is this lady?

"I'm in your group session. You made quite the entrance this morning," she chuckles.

"Oh, hi. I didn't catch your name," I prod her as I slowly walk beside her.

"It's Mabel," she answers warmly. "I just wanted to tell you that we're not allowed to jog or run during the walk time. Not that I could even if I wanted to," she chuckles again and limps forward.

"We can't run? Why?" Annoyance prickles over my skin and I rub my hand over my beard.

"A lot of people use exercise to get a bit of an endorphin rush, a little mini-high. In here, people get desperate to feel good again. Plus, walking makes you think more. It's more reflective. Anyway," she smiles at my scowl, "I don't make the rules, I just follow them. You can do what you want, but if you use this time to run you'll hear the same spiel from a counselor later." She warns gently.

This is fucking ridiculous. Get high from running. Seriously? What's next? No sugar because you might feel a rush? Instead of snapping at granny, I bite my tongue and smile back politely. Don't shoot the messenger, right? Especially not when she's a sweet, little old thing like her.

"Uh, thanks. I appreciate it." I look over at her curiously. What is she doing in a place like this?

"Heroin," her sweet voice interrupts my thoughts.

"I'm sorry?"

"I'm in for heroin addiction, I'm guessing you were

gonna ask. It's always the first question."

So much for a sweet, innocent granny.

"Oh, wow. That's intense." I walk alongside her.

"Well, it didn't start out that way. It started with an Oxycodone prescription. It ended with heroin." She answers sadly.

Holy shit, it's hard to imagine my walking partner with a needle in her arm. She must be in her late sixties or early seventies.

"Where you start is never where you end up, that's the thing with addiction," she continues softly.

"I'm sorry to hear that," I'm not sure what else to say.

"Don't be. I'm gonna be just fine."

My eye is caught by a flash of teal blue. A jacket in the crowd ahead. It's the jacket that catches my eye, but the long, flowing brown hair that I lock onto. She turns and looks back over her shoulder. Holly's beautiful blue eyes meet mine and I can't hear what Mabel is saying anymore.

"I'm sorry, I need to go," I interrupt her and quickly zigzag through the bodies separating Holly and I, without saying another word.

Ahead of me, Holly puts her head down and marches forward with more steam in her step. She's trying to avoid me, but after this morning's explosion I feel like we should clear the air. I mean, that's my excuse anyway.

"Hey, wait up," I call out. I know she can hear me, but she keeps pressing forward. I maneuver around a large gaggle of women clucking like hens and close the distance between us.

"Hey," I grab her arm, "I wanted to talk to you."

"I have nothing to say to you," she brusquely yanks her arm from my grasp and sets her jaw in determination. I easily keep up with her increased pace. If she thinks she's going to speed up and outwalk me, she's mistaken.

"Listen, I don't know what I did to upset you, but I'm sorry. Ok? I didn't mean to offend you this morning. Sometimes I'm not the best at expressing myself." I continue.

"You don't say," she snaps back, but some of the tension in her shoulders slides away and her pace slows slightly.

"It's true, look, icebreakers aren't really my thing."

"No shit," she answers.

"Like one time, I made a speech at my buddy's wedding. It was supposed to be touching. I talked about how when we went hunting, he'd open up about how he'd met the love of his life, even saying he'd met the woman he wanted to spend the rest of his life with," I explain.

"What's wrong with that?" She looks over at me and I almost stop walking when her face softens and her beauty radiates through. She's stunning.

"The problem was, I didn't know his wife was an animal rights type vegan and that when he went hunting with me, he'd told her he was just going camping as a cover story."

"Really?" Holly giggles and I can't help but smile back.

"Yeah, I mean, it's sort of funny now. But, at the time she had a nuclear meltdown and I was like the leper no one wanted to talk to. Like I said, even when I'm not trying, I offend people."

Holly laughs a little and slows her pace again. She looks so beautiful when she smiles. I mean, she's pretty damned sexy when she's pouting too. I imagine how her thick lips would feel crushed against mine. How they would look sliding down my body to my fat… I shake my head and focus my gaze on the mysterious girl beside me. I've never been one to get drawn in by a pretty face, to light up from a simple smile. Why is she so different?

"It sounds like you have bad luck," she pushes her hair back from her face and runs her fingers through the long locks. I want to wrap her hair around my hand while I make her mine.

"Oh, I don't know about that," I murmur. "I mean, who would've thought in a place like this I'd meet someone as beautiful as you. That's pretty lucky if you ask me."

Her freckles scrunch up on her ivory nose and she looks down at her feet. I've made her uncomfortable.

"Uh, anyway, I wasn't trying to say that I'm better than you because we grew up different." I try to change the subject back to my attempted apology.

"No? Well, your non-addiction to coke and your awesome, loving parents sounded better." Her voice runs cold.

"Hey, I've got my own shit. I bet everyone in here does. My family isn't perfect, ok? It's just not," I shake my head and try to stay in the moment, I don't want memories to overtake me, "it's just not the main thing I struggle with. I'm definitely not better than you. Just different."

Our shoes crunch against the twigs on the path below us. Holly looks up at me from under her eyelashes, like she doesn't fully trust me or my words.

"Ok," she says finally. Tension I didn't know I was

holding washes away with just that one word.

"Great," I smile. "Hey, we're both in here for coke, right? Maybe we can focus on our similarities. Help each other out with this thing, huh?" I ramble, happy to have reached a truce.

"Maybe," she answers tentatively. "Um, but right now the walk is over and I've got a class to go to. I'll see you in group tomorrow, ok?" She doesn't wait for me to answer, breaking off from the trail, she heads back to the front doors of Edgewood and doesn't look back.

I feel like we're doing a dance. Waltzing back and forth, one step forward and two steps back.

CHAPTER 9

Holly

I make my way down the hall to my room, trying to convince myself that my body is ready for sleep. I know I'm not tired. I just want to close my eyes and dream of him. Jake.

I want the freedom to talk to him, laugh with him, to kiss him. My heart flutters as the last thought lingers. What is it about him that makes me feel this way? I've been numb for so long, my world dulled by drugs and pain, I forgot how this feels. How a simple glance from his gorgeous eyes can make me happy and shy, at the same time. How a smile from his perfect lips can make a flush of heat rush through my body, igniting my soul.

Speaking of smiles, I can't hide the one stupidly pasted on my face right now. I'm getting funny looks from the other patients as I float through the hall like a girl who has finally been asked to the prom by her high school crush, but I don't care.

I turn the corner into my room and walk in through

the open door. They make us keep the doors open here during the day. I've been told that they do random inspections in the rooms to make sure no one is sneaking in drugs or booze. I guess it makes sense, but it still feels weird to know that just anyone could be rifling through my underwear or reading through my journal while I'm gone.

At least we get to close them at night. I'd never get any sleep with the bright light cascading into my room from the hall, like a spotlight on a prison tower. I fling the door shut and climb into bed. I'm so ready for sleep to overtake me. The days are long here. Like mercury, I feel myself melt away from my body, ready to reform into a new shape in my dreams.

I hear a noise from my closet and sit up in bed. The room looks different. I look around and realize that I'm in my childhood bedroom.

How did I...?

There's no time to question it because the noise in my closet is growing louder. I should run away, or scream, but I can't stop myself from opening the door. I know what's waiting for me before the door even opens, but I still gasp. My heart pounds rushing blood into my ears and my lungs struggle to take in air. I open my mouth to scream, but Knox steps forward from behind the door and clamps his hand over my mouth, muffling my cries with his meaty hand as he pushes me back against the wall with a thump.

"Shut your fucking mouth," he reaches behind him and pulls out his gun. The gun I shot him in the leg with. How did he get it back? I feel the cold metal nuzzle against my temple. Tears spring to my eyes as he cocks it.

"Make a fucking sound and I'll kill whoever comes in here, then I'll kill you." He sneers. I can't breathe. His hand is still locked over my lips and pressed up snugly under my nose, making it next to impossible to get any air.

Knox releases his icy grip from my face and pinches his fingers into the flesh of my arm. The flesh of my arm. The thought occurs to me. That's how I started thinking of myself when I was with him. Like my mind and body became separate entities. He could control my body, he could hurt my flesh, but he could never rule my mind.

"Knox, please," I whisper, knowing full well that he'll make good on his promise to kill anyone who walks in here.

"Shut the fuck up, bitch," he tosses me down and I tumble onto my bed. I slide back, desperate to put some space between us, until my back hits the wall behind me. I knew he would find me. I went to the furthest rehab center I could find, hoping to escape him. To give myself a chance to heal before I had to think of how to spend the rest of my life avoiding him. Damn it, I traveled to the Canadian west coast just to stay hidden. How did he find me?

"You thought you'd get away so easily, huh? I told you, baby girl, you ain't ever getting away from me. First, I'm gonna do you like you did me," he nods down to his leg.

I slap both my hands over my mouth to prevent the scream, that's welling up inside me, from escaping. His knee is bleeding down his leg, a fresh wound. Like I just shot him. My mind can't make sense of what I'm seeing, I shot him weeks ago. How is this happening? I watch in horror as the blood soaks his jeans and pools around his foot, slicking out over the floor.

"Knox, I'm sorry. Please…"

"I told you to keep your mouth shut!" He raises his hand and I cower, crunching myself down into a ball as I prepare myself for the impact of his gun. Nothing happens. I wait, my head tucked into my body, but he doesn't hit me. I peer up and his face is an inch from mine. I can see every scar, every wrinkle from years of drug use, I can smell the familiar tobacco and whiskey on his breath.

"I'm gonna blow your pretty little knee out, Holly. Then I'm taking you home with me. You got it? You're my property, bitch. The only way you're ever gonna leave me is in a body bag."

He presses the heavy muzzle of his gun against the top of my knee and I choke on my tears. Click! The distinctive cock of the gun warns me of what's to come. He can only hurt my flesh. My body. Not me. He can't hurt me. I won't let him hurt me. The thoughts repeat in my head like a mantra.

The door flings open and Jake pounces from the doorway and lands on Knox. How did he know? Jake cracks his fist across Knox's jaw, but he doesn't get control of his gun. The two of them struggle for power, rolling on the ground. Knox lifts the gun toward Jake's face, but loses control. Jake twists his hand and the two struggle for the weapon.

"Knox! No!" I shriek.

BANG!

My eyes spring open as I sit up in bed. The room is dark and quiet, where's Knox? And Jake? My heart thuds in my chest erratically and sweat prickles my brow. Was that…? I try to slow my panting and wipe away my tears with my knuckles. Was that just a dream?

I search the room, expecting Knox to jump out at me from the shadows. A shiver runs down the length of my body. It felt so real. Pulling the blankets around me tight, I lean back against the wall, trying to calm down. It was a dream. He's not here.

I know it wasn't real, but I can't shake my very real emotions. More than the sadness and more than the fear gripping my core right now, I'm overwhelmed by something else.

Shame.

How did I ever let that monster control me? How will I ever truly escape him? He hasn't found me here, so far. What about when my two months are up? What about when I go back to Everglades City? I've seen Knox track down dealers who owed him money. Men who've fled the state, thinking they'd pulled a fast one. I've never heard of one who got away. He always managed to track them down, he has eyes and ears working for him all across the country. And when he got his hands on someone who tried to fuck him over, someone who thought they could get away…

I shudder and pull the blanket tighter. If he ever finds me, death would be the least of my worries. Tears roll down my cheek and land on the mini blanket fort I've cocooned around me. I'll never get away. I'll never have my own life. I'm fucked. I drop my head against my knees and sob. It's over.

No.

The voice inside is little more than a whisper, but I heard it. I raise my head, sniffling. The whirlwind of worries still cyclone around me, but they aren't new. This little protest, now this is new.

No

This time my thought is louder. I won't lay down and give up. I'm not with Knox anymore and I'm not going to let him take the only thing I ever managed to keep as my own when he owned me; my mind.

"No!" I repeat the word to the darkness. I will get better and I will start my life over with a fresh mind and a healthy body. He won't stop me. He won't control me anymore.

No.

I lie back on the mattress and fix my blanket around me. It's time I broke free from this cocoon and showed the world my transformation. I'm a butterfly.

My head sinks into my fluffy pillow, cooled by the night air and I close my eyes. As soon as my eyelids flutter closed, Knox's face flashes in my mind.

"No!" I sit back up and yell to the night. This time, I don't feel the power of the word. Just the way I always used it, begging for something, for him, to stop.

I run my hands over my long hair, trying to soothe away my fears. There's no way that I can live like this. As long as Knox is in my head, I'll never be free from him, whether he finds me or not. I need to figure out a way to erase him from my mind. But how?

"I, like, never get scared," the memory of my sixteen-year-old friend, Roxy, floods my brain.

"Yeah right," I rolled my eyes.

"Even at night?" My twin sister, Heather asked her. "When you're all alone and it's dark?"

"Especially not then," Roxy flipped her luxurious blonde hair over her shoulder and sat up in her sleeping bag. My sister and I along with the other girls at our sweet sixteen sleepover leaned in to hear her secret.

"You're trying to tell me that you see some shadows, or hear some creepy noises and you never get freaked out by that?" One of our mutual friends, Gina, prodded.

"That's totally what I'm saying," Roxy tilted her head and looked down at us like a bunch of amateurs.

"How?" Heather asked her.

"Because," Roxy smirked, "you can't be scared and horny at the same time," she let the words hang, marinate in our teenage minds.

"Wait, what?" I asked.

"Ok, so, every time I start getting all nervous or feel a bit scared or whatever, I just force myself to think of the hottest guy I can picture. And then I let my fingers do the rest," she giggles.

"Ewww, you're gross!" Gina twisted her sun-kissed face in disgust.

"Oh, as if you've never masturbated. Gimme a break!" Roxy laughed, throwing her pillow at Gina.

"Keep it down guys! You're gonna wake up my parents," Heather had chided them.

I let the memory fade away, once again I'm surrounded by the darkness and my fears of Knox. "You can't be horny and scared at the same time," Roxy's voice echoes in my ears.

Lying back on my bed I get comfortable and close my eyes again. This time, when Knox's face pops up behind my eyelids, I push him away and force myself to think of the hottest guy I can imagine.

Jake.

His shaggy brown hair, his deep blue eyes. I suck in my bottom lip and let my fingers trail down my body. Jake's trim beard surrounding his pale pink lips. I think of each part of him. His face. His body. Like layers of an onion, the fear peels away as I submerge myself into the fantasy.

I slip my hand under my pajama pants and let my fingers travel across my thigh to my wet pussy. I let my mind indulge in the perfect movie in my head.

"You're so sexy," Jake murmurs, soaking me in as the warm water of the shower splashes down around us. I don't shy away from his gaze, instead I feel powerful.

"So are you," I whisper, letting my fingers trail down over his chiselled abs until my hand wraps around his thick cock.

Water droplets fall from his beard as he smiles down at me. He leans over and takes my rosy nipple in his mouth, I moan and let my head fall back under the water.

Under my blankets, my fingers find my clit, aching with desire and I rub my sensitive nub and think of Jake.

"I don't want to cum from your hand, I want to feel you around me," Jake growls in my ear and easily lifts me in his arms.

I slide my legs around his waist and he presses me back against the tile wall as his member lines up against my wet entrance.

In bed, I swirl my fingertip around my clit, breathing hard as my pleasure builds.

"I need to feel you in me," I tighten my legs around him, desperate to feel our bodies merge together.

Jake presses his cock against my lower lips and I open for him. He feels so good as every inch of him slides inside my willing pussy. I press my hips down, hungry to feel him fill me. I feel tight around him while he pumps his cock in me. I feel myself stretch to take his full girth as the hot water steams up the air around us.

Jake holds me close, never making me feel like I might fall. His grip is firm, but never painful. His strength makes me feel safe.

I throw my head back against my pillow, squeezing my eyes tight as my orgasm floods over me. "Oh, Jake!" I moan as I twist my head to the side. I pull my hand from my pants and snuggle into my bed as exhaustion finally overwhelms me. I imagine Jake lying behind me, his arm wrapped around me. Keeping me safe, and drift off into a peaceful sleep.

CHAPTER 10
Holly

I'm the first one here. I've never been this early for, well, anything. Especially not for group. I scan the circle of empty seats and pick mine. I pick the chair that's second down from where our counselor, Gavin, sits at the head of the circle.

It's a strategic move, about as complex as putting your backpack on the bus seat next to you in hopes that no one will ask to join you. No one wants to sit hip-to-hip with Gavin. It's uncomfortable, so I'm hoping by taking the next seat over, I can save that spot.

Warmth tingles through me as I nervously wait to see him walk through the door. Normally, if I have any time to kill before the session starts, I spend it staring at my feet or lost in thought as I gaze out the window. Today, I'm smiling like a goof at every person in my group therapy as they pop up in the doorframe. Only to scowl at them in disappointment for not being him.

Jake.

There's those damned butterflies again. Fluttering around my insides like I've never seen a man before. Honestly, I haven't. Not like him. Knox wasn't the only boyfriend I ever had, but he was the first man I was ever with.

My eyes drift back down to my shoes against the green carpet as unwelcome thoughts of him infiltrate my mind. Jake is like everything that Knox tried so hard to be, and more. Not just in looks. Not just how Jake's deep blue eyes shine with kindness where Knox's sharp black eyes would narrow with hatred. Not just how Knox's sinewy, ropy muscles made him look like someone who dug their way out of Alcatraz, where Jake's sturdy, built frame looks like he could protect me from everything. It's also how Knox needed to carry, and often use, a gun to demand respect. Jake commands the same just by walking into a room. His confidence is something I've seen before, but when you mix it in with his boyish charm and his scruffy, sexy face…

I squirm in my seat as heat rushes through my core and my pussy clenches. I need to get a hold of myself, I shake my head and my long hair slides lazily back and forth. My attempts at regaining self-control are short lived because Jake strolls into the room and a smile I didn't give permission to cross my face, tugs at my lips.

His eyes are locked on mine and my heart quickens as my breathing grows shallow. I force myself to look away, to drag my eyes from his handsome face and look somewhere, anywhere else. Mabel smiles knowingly at me from across the circle. She gives me a little wink, making deep creases from the scattered cobweb of lines around her eye.

Jake takes the seat next to me and I mentally high five

myself. It's the small things, the little wins that make the days bearable around here. That's what I tell myself about the surge of happiness flooding through me just because a guy I only met yesterday is sitting in the chair beside me. It would be ridiculous to get this excited for any other reason, right?

"So, uh, did you give anymore thought to my proposal?" Jake's deep voice cuts through my scattered thoughts and my focus lasers in on him.

The rest of the people shifting in the seats around me disappear. The room itself melts away. He's all I see. He's all I want to see.

"Um, proposal?" I lick my lips nervously as I try to push the image of him down on one knee, holding a diamond ring up to me from my mind.

Get it together, Holly!

I tuck my hair behind my ear and look up at him from under my lashes, waiting for the lips I fantasized about kissing me, to explain what he means.

Jake leans back nonchalantly in his seat and lets his eyes drift over me. "Yeah, what I mentioned yesterday. You know, about us trying to help each other through this?" His eyes shine with amusement as he waits for my mind to register what he's talking about. It doesn't. "Since we're both in here for the same addiction?" He continues after pausing long enough to see that my mind is drawing a blank.

"Oh, that!" I giggle. "Yeah, yeah, sure. I mean, technically, I think we're all supposed to help each other out in here. You know?" I fight hard to keep myself from looking as flustered as he's making me feel. The distinctive heat spreading over my cheeks is telling me I'm not doing that great of a job hiding it though. "But, I'd, um, I would like if we tried that."

Jake's smile makes the heat I was feeling in my cheeks rush through my entire body. I'm done with wondering how he can make me feel this way with just a look. It doesn't matter. He just does. For once, I'm going to stop overthinking and enjoy it.

"Get the fuck out of my seat, shithead," the room snaps back into crystal clear focus as Carl kicks the leg of Jake's chair.

What the fuck is this guy's problem? Jake's smile evaporates as he snarls up at the idiot who has been following me around Edgewood like a stalker since I checked in. Every woman has dealt with some version of Carl. The guy who talks too close. The guy looms around you like he's marking his territory. The guy whose creepy stares make you want to scrub a layer of your skin off in a hot shower. The shitty thing about a place like this is, I can't just leave at the end of the day and not worry about him. He's always lurking in the shadows, ready to assault my personal space with his delusional attempts to claim me.

"Listen man, because this is a one time warning, get the fuck out of my face. Now!" Jake lurches forward in his seat, snarling.

Across the room, Mabel interrupts the growing tension, "Carl, go sit yourself down and stop making a damned fool of yourself." Her sweet, granny face furrows with wrinkles.

Carl looks over his shoulder at her and then sneers down at Jake. I can see every muscle in Jake's arms tense as he looks like he's about to pounce from his seat.

Carl shrugs and rolls his eyes, "Whatever man. I don't

really want to sit by this little bitch anyway," he turns to find another seat and Jake almost knocks him off balance when he pops up to his feet.

"What did you just say?" He growls.

Carl turns back to face Jake. Their noses are little more than an inch apart. Jake's eyes narrow and his shoulders hunch forward as he balls his big hands up at his sides.

"Oh, I'm sorry," Carl answers mockingly, "you're right. My bad. I shouldn't have called her a bitch. Not when she's clearly a fucking slut," the words that I've heard Knox say more times than I can count feel like a slap to the side of the head. Carl shoves Jake's shoulders back, but he doesn't budge.

Jake's fist jabs up quickly, so fast that I don't have time to blink before it's over, and lands right under Carl's rib cage. The hiss of his breath leaving his body fills the room like a balloon being let go before it's tied off. The creep falls to his knees opening and closing his mouth like a fish out of water, trying to gasp of lungful of air. I grip the edges of my seat, watching as Carl sputters for his breath.

"Looks like you're the little bitch now," Jake's voice is rough like gravel.

"What are you doing?" All eyes in the room flicker over to the door to the office. Standing there, with his clipboard and a grimace is Gavin.

"Carl started it!" Mabel jumps in.

Gavin holds up his hand and she falls silent. "I don't care who started it, I'm ending it. Jake, Carl, let's go. You're getting discharged."

CHAPTER 11

Jake

From the waiting room, I can hear Gavin inside the office. Even if his voice wasn't as loud as it is, I'd have no problem listening since the door is open.

"I want them both out, not just Carl. This one has been nothing but a disruption since he walked in. I've been doing this long enough to know who's going to take their recovery seriously and who isn't," he yells.

I'm the only one seated in a line of chairs against the wall. Carl is already being discharged after everyone gave statements about who started that shit.

Clenching my jaw, I stare straight ahead as I eavesdrop. I can't catch a break. I mean, being in shit seems to be the only thing I'm good at these days. I don't care. I would drop that fucker again in a second for what he said.

I saw how it hurt her. How his pathetic name-calling clouded over her sky blue eyes as she hunched over, defeated. As if I was going to let him degrade her. Like fuck.

That asshole got what he deserved.

Now what's going to happen to me?

I hold my breath and tilt my head as I strain to hear the Director answer. "Gavin, it's not your job to decide who will recover and who won't. It's your job to break through to them and guide them through this program," she answers calmly.

"But, this is different…"

"The decision has been made. It's final. I won't argue with you. Carl is being processed to leave and Jake is staying. That's that."

I wait to hear my counselor's rebuttal, but instead I sit a little straighter in my chair as he comes huffing out of the office and storms past me. I stand up, not sure if that means I'm free to go, or what? Before I have a chance to overthink it, a tiny woman with huge, clunky heels comes clopping out to the waiting room.

She can't stand taller than five feet, and that's with the heels. Her severe, black pantsuit matches her severe, black hair that's neatly pulled back into a bun. Her oversized, round glasses make her look like an owl.

"Jake, please come into my office. We need to have a word," she holds out her hand to lead the way and I comply. For such a small woman, she is daunting. Her thin-lipped, no nonsense attitude is one I've seen many times with military brass.

I silently make my way into her cozy office. Sitting in the plush, leather chair in front of the desk, I soak in the array of diplomas framed on her wall as she makes her way to her seat.

"I'm Edna Morehouse," she begins, somehow sitting

evenly with me from across her large desk. Is she sitting on a phonebook back there? "I run this facility."

"Hi, Ms. Morehouse. I'm Jake Armstrong."

"I know." She nods. "And Edna is fine. We all use first names here. Even the staff."

"Uh, ok," I glance down at the file folder lying in front of her.

She opens the cover and looks inside at the first sheet. From where I'm sitting, I can see my name typed on the top.

"It's only your second day here, Jake. For you to end up in my office at all during your stay is never a good thing. I'd say that you're off to a rocky start, wouldn't you?" She blinks at me from behind her absurdly large glasses.

"You can ask anyone who was there, I punched that guy in self-defense. It's not like I started it, he attacked me," I dive into my justification.

Edna simply holds up her hand and I clamp down my jaw.

"Cool it, hot shot. I know what happened. And, as you no doubt heard, you're not being kicked out. At least, not today." She lets the threat hang ominously between us as she skims over the rest of my documents.

"I've looked at your file, Jake. It seems to me, that you might want to focus your attention on your program. I'm sure I don't need to remind you, if you don't graduate from rehab after your time here, you won't have a position to go back to in the Navy SEALs. Isn't that right?" Despite her stature, she seems to peer down her nose at me, like an owl on a branch. She has got to be sitting on a phone book.

"That's right," I sigh. She's right. If I don't get the green light from these people, then my career is over. The only job, scratch that, the only life I can ever imagine living would be nothing more than a memory. I shift in my seat and try to push the thought away.

"I'll do better," I answer. "I'll focus," I push the words through my gritted teeth.

"Good!" Edna beams cheerfully. I have to admit, I was more comfortable with the scowl. "I'm glad we could have this little chat then; you can go back to your routine now. I'm pretty sure it's almost lunchtime," she holds her hand up again, pointing to the door.

"Um, thanks." I stand up and make my way out.

"Oh, and Jake?" Her tone is cool; I turn around and her face has transformed back into a stone-cold stare.

"Yes?"

"I better not see you in here again, understand?"

I nod and walk out into the hall. I need to get it together. If they kick me out of here, that's it. I have nothing to go back to. My job, my friends, hell, my entire life has been the SEALs since I graduated high school. If I lose them, I lose everything.

CHAPTER 12

Holly

Is that him? No.

Disappointment floods through me as I watch another man walk into the dining hall and head over to the counter. Ever since Jake was hauled out of group this morning, I've been on pins and needles. Is he getting kicked out?

My heart sinks at the thought. I'll never be able to sleep easily, knowing he was shown the door because of me. Well, because of how Carl was acting toward me. Still, it wasn't his fault.

That's not the only reason you'll be upset, a little voice nags me.

I know it won't be. I know that if Jake leaves, even though I barely know him, even though we may never meet again once we're both out of here, I'll miss him.

I try not to let the thought linger. I don't like how it twists up in my gut and refuses to let go.

There he is! I jump up from my seat so fast that my chair almost topples backward. I steady it with my hand, also taking a moment to settle my nerves. Deep breaths.

Walking over to the counter on shaky legs, I try not to stare at him like a hunter narrowing a deer into their sights.

"Hey," I try to sound casual as I lean against the food counter where he's collecting his lunch.

"Hey yourself," he smiles back.

Damn, my heart is thudding like a drummer at a band audition.

"I saved you a seat, back there," I point to the little table stuffed in the back corner. I chose it purposely, hoping that, if Jake was staying, we would have a bit of privacy to talk. And, if it turned out he was leaving, it would give me a quiet place to cry.

"Looks good," he agrees. "Lead the way," he lifts his tray with the lunch special and follows me.

I can't help it, I'm giving my hips a little swing as I make my way through the crowded tables to the back. I don't have to turn around to know his eyes are on me, I can feel them.

We get settled in our seats and Jake nods at his plate, "Do you want some of these fries?" My eyes glide over salty, crispy, hot fries piled high beside his sandwich.

"No, that's ok."

"Are you sure?" He prods.

"Oh, ok, just one," I quickly rescue a fry from his plate and pop it into my mouth as Jake chuckles and shakes his head slowly.

"What?" I tilt my head waiting to hear what's so funny.

"Nothing, it's just, women always say they'll have just one fry and then they end up splitting them. I don't know why you do that," he takes a bite of his sandwich.

"I don't know either," I smile and grab another one of his fries.

I can see the twinkle of amusement in his blue eyes, but he doesn't say anything about it.

For a moment, I'm lost in him. It's amazing how just watching him can make the past, present and future blur around me like some kind of Van Gogh painting.

"Hey, I'm glad you waited for me. I wanted to find you. We need to talk," his voice interrupts the slowly swirling time warp and brings me back to the moment.

"Sure," I sit up straighter, "what do you want to talk about?"

"I'd like to apologize to you," he answers before taking another bite of his roast beef sandwich.

"Apologize?"

"Yeah, say sorry," he explains.

"I know what the word means," I laugh, "why are you apologizing to me?"

Jake puts his food down and looks into my eyes, my breath catches in my throat. His eyes, they're so intense. "I should've tried to deal with that asshole without, you know, being violent. I get the feeling that you've already dealt with enough of that from men," he stares into me. At least, that's how it feels. Like he's watching my secrets, my thoughts, my fears, all play out on a screen.

"You picked up on that, huh?" I look down at my ragged nails, trying to push down the swell of shame rising inside me.

"I did."

"How?" I force myself to meet his eyes again, even though it's unnerving. "I never told you about any of that, hell, I haven't told anyone here." I search his face.

"I'm pretty good at reading people. It's one of the things we learn in the SEALs. Knowing when people are lying, telling the truth, or hiding shit, can make all the difference between a mission being a success story or an epic failure."

My eyes dart back down, I grab another fry from his plate and think about his words. Makes sense.

"Do you want to talk about it?" His hand grazes against the edge of mine. His touch is a whisper, so light, but somehow reassuring.

"I don't think there's much to say, really. I ran away from home when I was seventeen. Went from a small town to Miami and it was just too much for me. I didn't know the first thing about surviving in the big city.
It didn't take long to feel like I was being swallowed whole." I look up at him and he nods, waiting for me to finish.

"So, when I met Knox, my ex," I explain, "it felt too good to be true. He was ten years older, had an amazing place, made amazing money, it all seemed like a fairy tale."

"But it wasn't?" Jake prods.

"Maybe like one of those Grimm Brothers ones. Where the happy endings are bleak and everyone has the plague." I force a weak smile.

"Doesn't sound good," Jake smiles at my attempt to lighten the mood.

"No," my smile slides off my face, "it wasn't good. Far from it." I pull another fry off his plate, but don't eat it. I just hold it as clips and glimpses of memories fight for a spot in my brain. "It wasn't good at all."

"He was violent?" Jake lowers his voice.

"Yes. Very. At first I did the whole 'he didn't mean to really hurt me that badly' thing. But it didn't take long to see that he did. He got worse and I never left because… I didn't have anywhere to go." I confess to the table.

"Why did you leave home? Were your parents violent too?"

"No," my voice is flat but firm. "They never laid a hand on me. Ever." I emphasize.

He nods slowly, "you don't have to tell me. I shouldn't be pushing you."

"No, it's ok. I left because," I swallow the hard lump in my throat, "I left because I could never undo what I did and it ruined my family. It ruined our lives. I couldn't take it anymore, the guilt, and the shame. Watching the sadness overtake their lives. Watching my neighbors shake their heads at me when I went out. Everywhere I went, I couldn't escape."

"I'm sure whatever you did couldn't be that bad," Jake soothes me.

Slow tears trail down my cheeks and my lower lip trembles, "It was," I whisper.

"Let me tell you, I know this from experience, sometimes it feels like we've done the worst thing in the world when we're in the middle of it, but it passes."

"No, not with this." My voice cracks.

"Why? What happened?"

"I have a twin sister, Heather." I swallow hard, "Had," I correct myself. "She died."

"I'm sorry," Jake grasps my hand, but I pull it back.

"She died, and I'm responsible. It's my fault she's dead." The tears slide over my cheeks and gather on my chin. "It's my fault."

CHAPTER 13

Jake

Holly drops her head into her hands and sobs uncontrollably. I gently lay my hand on her shoulder, trying to think of what to say. I have so many questions. What happened to her sister? How is it her fault? Obviously, she didn't mean to do her any harm, or she'd be in jail instead of here with me. As the tears drip from her palms and she chokes on her sorrow, it's easy to see that, whatever happened, Holly believes wholeheartedly that it is her fault.

"Hey, it's ok. Shhh, it's ok," I soothe her. She's in no state to answer a bunch of questions that aren't my business anyway. I want to pull her onto my lap with my arms wrapped around her tight and hold her against my chest until she feels better. However, in a place like this, you can't do that. It's considered inappropriate contact. It's a violation of one of their fifteen million rules around here. My mind flashes back to my meeting with the Director. I'm already on thin ice. If they kick me out of here, my career in the SEALs is through. I look around the nearly empty cafeteria and spot one of the counselors wading past the sea of chairs toward us. I instinctively pull my hand back. The last thing I need is another reason for them to give me the boot.

But, it's more than that, isn't it? The thought crosses my mind. This isn't about your career; you just don't want to leave her behind.

The realization fires through me like lightening. For the first time in my twenty-seven years, I've met someone I really want to get to know, and not just physically. I mean, let's not pretend I'm a saint, that's definitely part of it, but it's deeper than wanting to fuck her. I want to help her.

"Hey! You two! You're late for the activity. Let's get a move on!" A short, elderly woman with big, military style boots and khakis gives us our marching orders.

I choose to ignore the little dictator, turning my attention back to Holly. "Hey, are you going to be ok?" I murmur.

"Yeah, I will. I'm good," she manages to pull herself together remarkably quick, sweeping her thumbs over her tearstained cheeks like two wiper blades on a car window.

"Did you hear me?" The counselor stomps over to our table, it's impossible to tell if she's scowling or if her face is just wrinkled in such a way that she always looks miserable.

"We were just heading out," giving her the sweetest 'let-me-get-you-your-next-drink' smile I can manage.

Apparently, it was a scowl, because her deep lines shift and transform on her face as she tilts her head and smiles back at me.

"It's my fault, I was just blabbing about working in the Navy SEALs and totally lost track of time. I would hate to miss the... I'm sorry, what is the activity?" I lay it on thick. I know this woman's type. She might have a good thirty years on me, but she still wants to have a strong, young buck give her a smile that makes her melt.

"The what?" She blinks, like she's just awoken on a stage at a hypnotist's show with a crowd of unfamiliar faces smiling up at her. "Oh, uh, the activity. It's an Easter craft," she answers softly. Then, snapping her head back up straight, her lines return as she grabs a hold of her senses, "And you two are late! So, let's get this show on the road," she demands again.

This time we both listen and get up from our seats at our cozy table and follow her out of the dining hall.

"Easter craft?" I mumble to Holly. "Seriously?"

"Yeah, apparently, every week we have these mandatory group functions that we have to attend. It's so dumb." She rolls her pretty blue eyes.

"Nothing like mandatory fun," I smirk.

The counselor leads us into a large room filled with tables full of crafting supplies and surrounded by groups of patients. Each table is filled with every preschooler's dream of glitter, paints, stickers, pom-poms, glue and more. Well, doesn't this look... interesting.

I scan the faces of the present addicts in here. So many of them look unreasonably happy to be doing this right now. Like, this will be the highlight of their day that they write about on the sheet we have to turn in each night listing what we liked, hated and learned from our day in rehab. It's just one more way I can't relate to so many of these people. Not only are they in here because they let drugs or alcohol destroy them, and everything they held dear, but now they're so deliriously happy to find meaning in everything, that simple things like compulsory craft time brings genuine pleasure to their lives.

My eyes flicker back to Holly. I almost burst out laughing at the twisted look of pained disdain on her face. It's like I can see the thoughts running through my brain playing out like a projector on a movie screen across her milky complexion.

I might not be able to relate to these guys, but this girl? The one right I can't stop thinking about. The one whose scent drives me wild. The one who I've only just met, but feel like I've known since we were kids, I get her.

"Ok, enough dilly-dallying now. You both take a spot at that table back there," the silver-haired woman points across the room to the only table with less than ten people crowded around it. "We've got to get started."

"Sure," I start to walk away, "wait." I turn back to face her and watch as her deep scowl evolves into a softer gaze again. "What is it we're supposed to do?"

"Oh, um, the activity is to take one of the cardboard eggs at your station and decorate it to represent your truth." She explains, like she's actually speaking English.

"My truth." I repeat.

"Yes."

"And, these are… Easter eggs?" I try to make the connection, but can't.

"Yes."

"So, are we hiding our 'truth' around the building and doing an egg hunt or something?" I'm honestly not even trying to be sarcastic. Although, I can see it's not being taken that way.

"No, of course not." She snips at me.

"Are we donating these eggs to children or something? For them to enjoy?" I grasp at straws to make sense of what possible association this could have with Easter.

"No! No egg hunt, no donations. It's just Easter eggs of your truth. Now, get to your table and get it done before you run out of time," she peers down at her wristwatch, reminding me of the rabbit from Alice in Wonderland always worrying about being late.

I look around me for Holly, but see she's already joined the table we've been assigned, so I clamp my jaw shut and head over. I guess it doesn't matter if I understand the reasoning. Or, if there actually is any. It's time to spend beside her, and that's time well spent.

"You ready to glitter your truth?" I slide in beside her at the table with a smirk. "Oh, look at this!" I mockingly point to the pile of art crap in the center of the plastic, pop-up table, "If glitter isn't 'truthy' enough, you can put rhinestones on that shit!" I pick up a package of dollar store fake jewels.

Holly laughs loud enough to deafen the scowls of other participants at the table. I don't give a fuck about them, or what they think of me. I'm only focused on one person, and if I can make her laugh after how hard she was crying in the cafeteria a little while ago, well that's a win.

"Ok, I know it sucks, but let's just do it. Who knows, maybe it'll help out a couple of lost coke-heads like us," she smiles up at me sweetly and it takes every ounce of physical restraint I have, in every fiber of my muscles, not to kiss her. God damn it! She's so beautiful.

She doesn't wait for me to stop staring at her like a man who's been shipwrecked and hasn't seen a woman in a decade. Instead, she grabs some paints, an egg, and gets to work.

I pick up a cardboard, unmarked egg shape and stare at it blankly. What the fuck am I supposed to draw on this thing? My truth. Whatever the hell that means. Like I'm going to paint my deepest pain or my biggest desires on the side of a pretend egg. Anger wells up inside of me at the thought.

I can't believe my brothers are back in Virginia Beach doing real shit, like fighting terrorism and defending our soil in operations most people won't ever hear about and I'm here doing this. This fucking stupid craft. Like I'm a six-year-old boy instead of a twenty-seven-year-old man.

Fine. They want my truth? Then the truth is what they'll get. I grab a paintbrush and dab it into the paint.

Time evaporates as I create my masterpiece. With a few flicks of the wrist, I admire my rudimentary artwork with a grin. Sure, it's no Da Vinci painting, but it'll do the trick.

"Time's up!" The counselor who rounded us up like a couple of stray cattle chirps. "I'm going to come around and collect your eggs in this Easter basket, one-by-one. I'm going to ask that you share the truth, your truth that you decorated on your egg with the group, please." She stands up, with a giant wicker basket in tow.

My mind blurs out the monotony of listening to person after person explain their biggest dreams and aspirations. The sheer volume of people who put down "getting clean" as their "truth" tells me, again, how little I have in common with these people.

Finally, the scowling counselor makes her way to our table, collecting each egg in her basket like a reverse Easter bunny. When she asks Holly what her truth is, my hearing finally kicks back in. My focus lasers in on her as she explains the little puppy dog that she's drawn on the side of her egg.

"I, well, I guess even in my darkest times, and I mean the absolute worst moments I've ever lived, I've always felt a deep connection with animals." She speaks to a room of nodding heads. "So, I guess, my truth is that I want to do something to help animals as much as they've helped me," she answers, placing her egg in the basket.

"Perfect," the counselor gives her a flash of a smile and then turns her attention to me. "And what is this?" She points to my design.

"That's me," I explain the little boy I've painted on the side of my egg.

"What are you doing?" She looks at the rough artwork quizzically.

"I'm smashing your basket of eggs," I point to the cracked shells and exposed yolks spread around my egg in a mess.

"What? Why? How is this your 'truth'?" Her voice raises with anger.

"Because, I truthfully think this activity is a stupid waste of time. If I was a little boy, and you sent me a basket of your Easter eggs of sadness, then I'd smash the shit out of them. And," I pause with a smile, "that's the truth."

Laughter erupts around me, but the only person I can really hear is Holly. Her quiet chuckle is, by far, the loudest in the room to me. I don't care about the angry lines forming in the counselor's face, or whether or not I'm going to have to sit in Ms. Morehouse's office again today, the only thing I care about, the only thing that matters, is the moment of happiness I've managed to bring to Holly. No matter how fleeting it is, it was worth it all.

CHAPTER 14

Jake

The desert wind swirls around me, the sand attacking my exposed skin like a million, tiny hailstones. That's how I think of it anyway, even after living in Virginia Beach for years, it still reminds me of the brutal Colorado winters I grew up with.

Why am I here?

I don't have time to ponder, my hands are suddenly weighed down by my Colt M4A1, and my tactical gear adds gravity to my body. I need to move.

My feet grit against the grainy dirt as I quietly enter the dark building. It's eerily calm. They know we're here. It won't do them any good though, we've got them surrounded.

With my night vision goggles, I can see the blurry details of the house. The first floor is clear. I sweep each room, my gun held out at the ready, as I search for our target through a filter of green. The night vision makes it feel like a video game.

I throw up the hand signal and make my way up the stairs.

We've been briefed that this building has at least four floors. We have to sweep them all. We have to take out our target. No exceptions.

I quietly creep down the hall, into the first bedroom. My partner is on my heels, ready to cover me from anyone stupid enough to try to attack us from behind.

Empty.

Next room is the same. As I inch toward the last door on this floor, I hear a woman say "Shhh!" They're hiding in this room. But is he? I can hear them cowering. His family. I hope he's not using them as a human shield. It wouldn't surprise me though, you don't get to be the head of the most powerful terrorist organization in the world living by a strict moral code.

I open the door, I can see the women and children huddled against the back wall. The mothers are using their bodies to shelter their babies. I don't care about them. I'm not here for them. I sweep the room, he's not here.

Suddenly, I'm blinded. I can't see anything! I rip off my night vision goggles to see that a bright light has been turned on in the room, making them useless. There's no time for my eyes to adjust to the light, because standing two feet from me is a boy, maybe eight years old. There's a burning rage in his eyes and a snarl on his face as he points the gun in his hands at my face.

BANG!

Chaos erupts. Children and their mothers scream. They try to rush the door, but they can't. My guys have them covered. One of the mothers crawls across the floor, wailing. She makes her way over to the body on the floor. The lifeless boy, who only a second ago was ready to kill me. Dead. His body floods the floor with blood. The blood of a child. Her screams grow louder and louder as the blood pools around him.

"Fuck!"

My heart is jackhammering in my chest as I shoot up in bed. Cold sweat trails down my face and my panting fills the night air.

"It was a dream. A dream." I repeat the phrase like a mantra. However, I know different. I know that this time it was a dream, but that's because I already lived the nightmare.

I swing my feet over the edge of my bed, letting them rest on the cool tile floor as I regain my senses. My heart rate begins to slow to a normal pace. I wipe the sweat from my face with the back of my hand and stand up. Giving my arms a shake, I try to push the thoughts back down.

The clock on the end table says it's a little after three in the morning. I don't even need to check it to know that. It's always the same. The dream is the same. The time I wake up is the same. The reality is the same.

I know I'm not getting anymore sleep tonight. Normally, I would take a shower, maybe do some reading to kill time before the daily grind starts back up. Tonight, I feel trapped in this tiny room. I've never wanted coke this much. I need a distraction, and cocaine has been perfect for that. The endless rush of energy it's given me has made these three-hour power naps I've been calling 'a night's sleep' bearable. A little white powder can numb these thoughts haunting me every night. It isn't the coke I'm addicted to, really, it's the escape.

I pull on a pair of jeans and a t-shirt and step into my shoes with my bare feet.

A walk will do me good. I just need to get outside these four walls. I need to give myself something to do.

I make my way down the empty hallway. It's weird to see this place so dead. All day long, there's always a couple hundred patients milling around. There's no escape from the shuffling bodies, clogging the halls as they make their way to lectures or therapy sessions like zombies on the Walking Dead.

Tonight, there's none of that. It's just me. For a moment, I consider taking a little jog up the empty hallway. However, I know they have a night person who roams around here to make sure all the addicts stay nestled in their beds. I remember how Mabel, the old lady from my group therapy sessions, told me that they frown upon people doing exercise. That they think it gives you a mini-high.

No. I won't jog. When I run into the night guard, I'm sure I'll already have explaining to do for being out of my room, I don't need to add another layer by getting into trouble for doing some minor cardio too.

I push my hands into my pockets and shake my head, annoyed at the stupidity of some of these rules. Before I know it, I realize that I'm approaching Holly's room. I stop in my tracks. I shouldn't be here.

But I am.

My heart rate quickens again, but this time it's not from fear. From the crack under her door I can see light spilling out across the hall floor. A rush of adrenaline shoots through me.

She's awake.

At least, I assume so. I look down the hall behind me. Should I? I slowly close the distance between her door and my body. I shouldn't, right? I should keep walking. Talk to her in the morning. I know this, yet I still approach her room. I don't remember my feet stopping, or making a fist, but my knuckles lightly rap on her door somehow. I tilt my head and listen.

Nothing.

Damn. I guess she is sleeping. The air feels like it's deflating from my lungs as I start to move away. It's for the best. I don't need to get in the kind of trouble that going into her room in the middle of the night will surely bring. And, I'm not talking about getting my knuckles rapped by the Director either.

"Who is it?" Her voice is little more than a whisper, but I'm sure I heard it.

I stand up taller and walk back to her door. "It's Jake," I whisper back.

CHAPTER 15

Jake

I can hear her feet hit the floor and pad over the tile as she makes her way to the door. When she opens it, the bright light casts down from the ceiling, glowing around her like a vision from heaven. She looks like an angel. My eyes slowly travel over the formfitting t-shirt she's wearing as a pajama top. Her perky, little tits are pressed up against the fabric as her rock hard nipples are begging to be freed. She tugs the shirt down over her creamy thighs, but it barely covers the glimpse of her sexy underwear. She's an angel alright. She looks like one of those Victoria's Secret models.

"What are you doing here?" She looks nervously over my shoulder into the hallway.

"I couldn't sleep. I didn't mean to come here, but then I saw your light on," I whisper back.

She bites her lip. Her perfect, plump, pink lip and my cock stirs. God, the dirty thoughts I've already had about that pretty mouth of hers.

"Ok, come in," she holds the door open and I walk in. I hear the distinctive click of the door closing behind us. I can only go by my hearing because Holly turned off the bedroom light. We're both standing in darkness. I can hear her breathing quicken and my cock begins to get hard.

"What are you doing?" I murmur.

"Just a sec," I hear her walk past me.

Click! A subdued light casts across the space as she turns on the small lamp on her bedside table.

"If you came here because you saw my light, then the night patrolman might do the same. I can't risk getting caught with you in here," she explains.

Makes sense.

I nod, silently, as my eyes trail over every inch of her like my tongue longs to. "Good idea," I finally manage the words.

"Why are you here? Is something wrong?" I can't pry my eyes off of her. She's perfection. The way her shirt rides up as she takes a breath, exposing her silky legs. Legs I've already imagined wrapped around my waist, or my head. Holly looks down and pink flushes over her cheeks as she seems to remember, for the first time, what she's wearing. She hops into her bed and pulls her blanket over her. She casts her eyes down at her buried legs, like she's studying the comforter's pattern with deep interest.

"Sorry," I look away, a pang of guilt hits me in the gut for making her feel self-conscious. "I swear," I hold up my hands, "I didn't come here for that," I try to explain.

"No?" Her blue eyes meet mine.

"No."

"Then what did you come here for?" She raises her chin and looks me straight on, sticking out her bottom lip like I've insulted her somehow.

"I... I don't know. I couldn't sleep, so I guess I just really wanted to see you. Being around you, talking to you, seeing you, it makes me feel better."

"You can sit over here," she pats the space on the bed next to her. I don't need more than that. The mattress sinks under my weight as I sit beside her.

"I couldn't sleep either," she confesses. "I have a lot of bad dreams."

"Yeah, me too."

"Really?" I can feel her scrutinizing my face, but I can't look at her. I can't tell her about the image that haunts me every night. Instead, I swallow hard and try to bury it inside.

"You know, when I was younger I had a friend that told me something kinda interesting," she changes the subject.

I look back at her and she gazes up at me from under her eyelashes.

"What's that?" God, she smells amazing. The way she's looking at me right now, it's astonishing that I haven't kissed her.

"She told me that it's impossible to be afraid and horny at the same time," she smiles slyly at me and my cock throbs against my jeans.

"Is that a fact?" My voice grows thick and I move closer to her.

"It is." She breathes.

"I think I'm going to have to test that out," I wrap my hand around the back of her head and crush my lips against hers. She parts her mouth eagerly and our tongues collide. She tastes sweet. Like there's still some innocence behind her wall of pain; innocence that I'd like to claim.

Her hands quickly slide over my shoulders and down my back. Her movements are frantic, desperate, like she needs this as much as I do. Maybe even more.

My fingers trail down to the edge of her shirt and I pull it up, breaking our kiss when I reach her chin, then I tug it off her sexy body. I throw back the blanket she tried to hide under and shamelessly soak in every inch of her almost naked frame.

"Take yours off," her voice is hoarse with desire. I quickly rip off my own shirt and toss it to the floor beside hers. She drinks me in and I move over to the edge of the bed, leaning my back against the wall, I pull her on top of me so she's straddling my rigid cock, still bound by my jeans.

I lick down the side of her neck and trail my tongue down over her collarbone and over her chest. When I pull her rosy nipple into my mouth, she throws her head back and grinds down against me, driving me wild. I want to make her mine. To feel her sweet pussy clench around me as I fuck all of her fears, her sadness and her pain away. I want to make her forget everything that came before me, to make her feel like a virgin again, as her walls stretch around me, letting me take what's mine.

I push my fingers under the flimsy fabric of her underwear and part her lips with my finger as I suck her nipple into my mouth. Holly groans and presses herself down onto my hand. I can feel her excitement, she's wet. However, I know from experience that she's needs to be soaked if she's going to enjoy every inch of what I have to give her.

I free her nipple from my mouth and look in her beautiful eyes, "Stand up," I growl.

"What?" She looks puzzled, but I guide her to her feet and she complies. She stands in front of me, looking unsure of herself.

"Lean your arms on the wall," I instruct her. As she does, her sweet pussy moves less than an inch from my face. I can smell her sweet juices and I salivate.

"Don't move," I order her and pull her panties over her plump ass, tugging them down to just above her knees.

I don't waste any time, cupping her ass with both hands, I pull her toward my needy mouth and dive my tongue into her neatly-trimmed pussy.

"Ahhh," she squirms in my hands and I pinch my hands into her flesh and I hold her in place.

I lick her from her center to her sensitive little nub, holding her tight while she wriggles in my hands. Flickering my tongue against her, I feel her thighs quiver on either side of my face as I eat her out. I keep licking her clit, relentlessly in pursuit of her orgasm until I no longer need to press her into my mouth. Instead, she starts grinding her hips, pressing her pussy deep against my face, chasing her pleasure from my tongue.

I look up the length of her body above me. I watch as her perky tits bounce a little each time she thrusts her hips forward. I flatten my tongue against her clit and slide it over her until she's trembling against me. Her breathing is ragged and she drops her head to the wall supporting her and squeezes her eyes shut while she lets me rack her body with ecstasy.

"Ooohhh, fuck!" She whimpers, her sweet nectar floods her pussy and I lap it up as she shakes with bliss.

Suddenly, her knees buckle and she unexpectedly crumples into my lap. "Are you ok?" I whisper, pulling her toward me.

"More than ok. That was fucking amazing," she breathes.

"I'm glad," I smirk.

"No, I mean," she looks up at me shyly, "no one has ever done that for me before," deep red burns across her cheeks at her confession.

I raise an eyebrow, "Really?"

"It's true," she mumbles.

I knew I would make her mine. "Now, how about I do something for you?" Her nimble fingers quickly pry open my jeans and she reaches in, wrapping her hand around my ready cock.

I stifle my laugh as I watch her eyes grow wide, "Are you serious?" Her hand explores my thick dick and her eyes drop down to soak it in, like she can't believe her sense of touch alone.

"Don't worry, I'll go slowly," I smirk.

"Oh my god!" Her blue eyes grow even bigger as she examines the ten inches I'm going to stuff inside her.

Holly shuffles back on the bed, hovering her mouth over my ready cock. I can feel the heat of her breath on my skin, teasing me. I groan as she slowly licks her lips in anticipation. She lowers her mouth, her lips surround the head of my dick.

Squeak, thunk, squeak thunk.

"Shit! What was that?" Holly's eyes are still opened wide, but this time in sheer terror. I heard it too. The distinctive sound of squeaky sneakers making their way up the hall. It's the staff doing the nighttime rounds.

We're fucked.

I jump from the bed with Holly in my arms and lie her back down against the mattress, throwing the blanket over her naked body. Quickly, I pick up my shirt, flick off the lamp on the table next to her, and hop across the room silently. I snugly slide into the little closet at the end of the room just as there's a rap at the door.

"Hello?" Holly answers too loudly and too full of emotion for someone who's supposed to be sleeping.

I hear the door open and a female voice is muffled but I can still make her out, "Everything ok in here?"

"Yeah, why?" Holly sounds guilty.

"I saw a light from your room and thought I heard some noise. Are you ok?" The woman persists.

"Yeah, I just went to the bathroom, no biggie," Holly laughs nervously.

"If you're sure?"

"I am."

"Ok, then. Sleep well."

I hear the door swing shut and Holly lets out a deep breath. I wait before moving a muscle. I'm not sure if the staff has left or if she's hovering outside Holly's door.

I hear Holly slide out of bed and make her way over

to the closet. She pulls open the door with fear tattooed across her face. "That was close," she hisses.

It was. Too close. If I got caught in here, Holly and I would both be kicked out. That would mean the end of my career, the end of her treatment, but most importantly: the end of us.

"You need to leave," she looks up at me apologetically. My balls ache and, for a split second, I entertain the thought of getting caught and all that comes with it, if it means fucking her. Somehow I shake my head free from the thought.

No. I'll go back to my room and take care of myself. It's not worth the price. Not when it could cost me her.

I nod, and silently slip out of her room, down the hall, and back into my own bedroom. I can still taste her juices on my face, see her lips hovering over my cock, and feel her heat on my skin. I reach down under the blanket and take my dick in my hand. It's not even close to being as good as it was with her, but it'll have to do.

CHAPTER 16

Holly

"I can't believe it's already been a month," Jake mumbles, staring out the floor-to-ceiling window overlooking the parking lot. "We're halfway through this," he pries his eyes from the cars filling up the usually empty spaces, and glances over to me.

"I know, it's incredible," I agree. I can't help the smile that spreads over my face when I look at him. It's automatic. I've never met someone who made me feel this happy.

I'll have to add it to the long list of things I've denied myself over the years. Happiness, sobriety, comfort, love. I guess I never thought I deserved any of it. I allowed a terrible mistake that took my sister's life, to steal mine as well. I realize now, she wasn't the only one who died that night. I may have still been walking and breathing, but I was only existing. A shell. My spirit left me that night along with hers. It's only now, in this past month, that I've felt it return.

"Do you see your parents yet?" Jake nods toward the groups of people exiting the multitude of vehicles outside.

I scan the crowd, but don't recognize anyone. "Nope, not yet."

Those of us who are at the midway point of treatment are getting a visit from our families today. Before this, we hadn't had any contact with them. I guess the idea is that they want us to focus solely on ourselves and our recovery, not the possible baggage that many of us have with our loved ones.

"I don't see mine either," Jake looks out the window quickly, as if to reconfirm what I just said.

Butterflies erupt into chaos inside me as my eyes travel slowly down his face. His deep blue eyes that stop time and blur the world around us, his pale pink lips under his sexy brown beard. My mind flashes back to the night he snuck into my room. To how amazing his lips felt between my thighs. Heat flashes through me, flushing my cheeks, and I bite my bottom lip. That was the most amazing feeling I've ever experienced.

I hate that we decided to cool it after that night. After almost getting caught, it was too close for comfort. We promised each other to practise some self-control and not have any more midnight visits. I've been tempted to go back on that promise every single night. However, I think it's helped us both a lot to put more of our effort into this program and less into sneaking around. Even Jake, Mr. Tough Navy SEAL, seems to be taking it more seriously.

"Hey, what's on your mind?" Jake smirks down at me.

I look down at my feet, knowing I'm a shit liar, "Nothing, why?"

"Nothing, huh?" His voice is like velvet. "Your eyes just glazed over and you're blushing like crazy," I can hear the amusement in his tone. "It doesn't look like nothing from here," he presses me.

I look up at him from under my eyelashes, feeling shy. "That night," I whisper, determined to keep our secret from the nosy crowd of patients surrounding us.

"I love when you bite your lip like that," Jake murmurs. I didn't even realize that I was doing that. I immediately push my mouth closed and feel my skin burn with a deeper shade of red. "God you're sexy," he continues.

"Thank you," my voice is weak, but my heartbeat is pounding strong. I can hear it rushing the blood in my ears.

Jake steps toward me, closing the already small gap between us, I breathe him in. He smells like coffee and a walk through a cedar forest after a heavy rain.

"I think about it every single day. And, when we get out of here," he drops his voice so his words can only reach my ears, "I'm going to make that night look like amateur hour." My nipples pebble under my shirt and my clit aches for him.

"I can't wait," I whisper, tucking my hair behind my ear, I look up into his face. I've never met a man who can make me wet from a simple look.

Jake looks around and takes a step back. The foot of space feels like a canyon between us, but I understand why he has to move away. We always have to be aware of how close we stand, how often we talk, how long we stare. Otherwise, it could mean the end.

"Hey, there's my folks," Jake's voice returns to normal as he points to an elderly couple making their way to the building.

I scour the growing crowd at the front door for my own mother and father, but can't make them out.

The receptionist out in the lobby buzzes open the front doors and the families begin to shuffle inside the main building.

"I should go see them," Jake smiles down at me. "See ya later, ok?"

"Ok," I smile and watch him strut across the lobby to greet his parents. They're much shorter than him, even his father stands a good six inches smaller than he does. Of course, it's not hard to feel like some kind of elvish creature next to Jake. He's at least six-two, but feels a lot taller from the way his heavy, cut muscles fill his towering frame.

They walk away down the hall together and I redirect my attention to the crowd pouring into the building. My eyes laser in on the unfamiliar sea of faces, carefully watching each stranger enter the facility until it dries up into a slowly trickling stream. I'm not sure how long I've been standing here motionless, watching. My head twists like an owl, desperately searching for my parents. Instead, I see the last few people enter the building and cheerfully greet their daughter at the door. It's the reception I haven't had in years.

Tears fill the corners of my eyes and my gut knots as I spin around on my heel to look back out to the parking lot. I stare for too long, with my breath held, silently hoping that they're just late to show up. That they're just slow to get out of their car. That there's some reason that they didn't show up, other than the truth.

I gaze out the window like a puppy in a shelter for

longer than I should. The realization finally hits like a tsunami, drowning me in despair. They aren't here, and they aren't coming.

They haven't forgiven me. Even now, after I've tried to put my life back together and get clean. After so many years of us being apart.

They still don't love me.

CHAPTER 17

Jake

I lead my parents to one of the rooms normally reserved for group therapy. Today, they've been reassigned as a place for patients to talk to their family members, although not privately. I look around the room at the other people I've come to know sitting in here with their loved ones. It's not exactly an intimate setting where you can pour out your soul. Not that I want to do that anyway.

I was annoyed when I found out I couldn't just take my folks down to my room where we could grab some chairs and chat for a few hours. The staff here informed me that it's another one of the rules that all visits are confined to public areas only. That way the roving counselors can check in on all of us and make sure nothing is getting too out of hand.

I think the real reason is that they don't want people who haven't seen their husbands or wives in over a month to turn this into a conjugal visit. I quickly look around the room for some empty seats. I spot a few available over by Mabel. I have to give her a second look, because her transformation is jarring. Usually she can be found shuffling down the halls in slippers, no matter the time of day, and baggy sweaters that could double as dresses. Today, she's all dolled up, in a pale yellow dress. Her white hair is pulled up into a bun with tiny tendrils framing her face, like smoke rising up from a campfire. She's even wearing makeup and, on her feet, where a fuzzy pair of pink slippers normally reside, she's got a black pair of flats on.

Sitting next to Mabel is an old man wearing a sports jacket and dress pants. From the way he looks at her, I know without a doubt in my mind, that the reason we need to have our guests in public places is exactly the reason I suspected. They don't want sweet, little Mabel and her horny husband getting filthy on their watch.

"Let's grab those seats," I point to the ones I've scouted and my parents comply. Mom seems pretty chipper; a big smile is pasted on her face. I know it's her default mode that's she's slipped into right now, she's not actually deliriously thrilled to be at a rehab facility visiting her son. She's just putting on a brave face. I glance over at my father. It's a lot more than I can say for the old man; his mouth is twisted down and his eyebrows are furrowed together as he glances around like he's looking for someone to yell at.

"I'm glad you came," I smile. "I know it was a really long way to travel. What do you think of British Columbia?" I make small talk.

"Oh, Jake, it's really beautiful. It reminds me of when I was a little girl and your grandfather took the family on a trip down the Pacific Coast Highway. Just breathtaking, isn't it Don?" Mom tries to pull my father out of his funk and into the conversation.

"I guess." He looks at his hands. He won't look at me. When they first got here, I gave Mom a hug and held out my hand for Dad, but he wouldn't shake it.

"How's my superstar brother, Cameron, doing?" I plod onward, ignoring my father's radiating anger.

"Oh, he got drafted by Miami," Mom answers excitedly. He and Chelsea will be moving on down to Florida next month. It's so exciting, isn't it Don?"

"Sure is," Dad's voice is flat. He's still staring down at his palms, like he never realized he had hands before and he's trying to figure out how they work.

I take a peek around the room to see if any other families are having as much fun as mine. Most of them are either murmuring closely like Mabel and her man, or happily chatting away like the others in here. Not one is slumped over and sullen like my father.

"What about you Jake? I've been so worried about you," my mother's eyes fix on mine. I can see she's not lying, under the layer of makeup she's wearing, dark bags are still visible beneath each eye.

"I'm really doing well, Mom. Please, don't worry." I answer truthfully.

"It's my job," she smiles at me and, for the first time since she walked in here, it's genuine.

"Is this a good program?" She continues, "Is it working?"

I will spare her the details about how long it has taken me to feel like this has been anything but a waste of time, rehab-wise. Obviously, my time here with Holly has been anything but. However, I don't think she wants to hear about that either. Especially since Holly and I don't have a real future together. The idea pains me, and I push it away.

Instead, I remember how, about a week ago, we had a guest speaker that put it all into perspective for me. Instead of the usual array of ex-addicts they parade in here to give us speeches about how much better their lives are now, they had a guest speaker I could relate to. A soldier.

Sure, he was a Canadian, so not exactly a SEAL, but we're all brothers in arms. I sat up straighter when he talked about how his addiction started after he returned from duty. One thing he said really stuck with me, "Addiction is tricky, it starts for one reason. In my case, I needed to get out of my own head sometimes. However, even though it starts because of one particular cause, it always continues for another. It morphs. Takes you over. Until you're not using because of shit you experienced or saw anymore. You're using because you're an addict."

That hit home for me.

I look up at my mother, she's watching me closely. How many nights of sleep have I stolen from her? How much worry, how much anguish, and how much sorrow have I exchanged for her rest?

"Mom, I really am doing well," I finally answer. "I didn't think I needed help when I first came, but I know I'm in the right place now. It's working," I smile. "My name is Jacob Armstrong and I'm an addict," I smile weakly, trying to make light of the confession.

"That's wonderful to hear, Jake. Not that you're an addict, of course, but that it's working. I'm so happy to hear that it's working. I've been praying for you." Tears brim her eyelids and she clasps her hands together in front of her heart.

"Thank you, Mom."

"Don, did you hear that? Jake's getting better." She urges my father to participate, but he just juts out his jaw in silence. "Donald, will you stop sulking and speak to your son," she raises her voice, clearly feeling as annoyed as I am by my father's attitude.

"I'm not sulking. I have nothing to say to him," he spits out the last word like it burned his tongue.

"Donald Armstrong, I told you not to do this," my mother leans into him as she hisses her words quietly. I know that the idea of our family making a scene horrifies her.

"I'm not doing anything," my father pouts. "I told you I never wanted to come here. You can sit there and act like everything's all better just because he says he's an addict or whatever. But, that don't make a lick of difference to me," his voice is starting to fill the room.

"Keep it down, Don," my mother scolds him. I look around the room, and other families are trying hard not to notice our family scuffle.

"Why? Why should I keep it down, huh? So, people in this room don't know what a failure our son is? So, they don't find out how much he humiliated our family? How he got caught with cocaine by the police and he decided to run away, like a coward?" A wave of crimson is rising up his neck and splashing onto his cheeks as his voice keeps getting louder.

"I'm sorry for that, Dad," I admit. "I'm ashamed of what I did, there isn't a day that goes by when I don't think about it. Trust me," I try to jump in.

"Oh, you're sorry? Well, then that makes it all ok, doesn't it? Did you hear that, Bev? He's sorry. All fixed." He claps his hands together like he's brushing of dirt.

"Don," my mother drops her head from the now staring eyes of other families in this room, "stop."

"No, I won't." Dad hops to his feet abruptly. "I won't sit here and act like everything is ok, just because he's sorry. Or act like it's all water under the bridge just because he wants a participation medal for being here. It doesn't change anything!" He points in my face, "It doesn't change what you did."

I jump to my feet and stare my father down as anger licks at the back of my throat. "How about instead of pretending that what I did was ok, you just pretend not to be such a shitty excuse for a father. Try that on for your first acting lesson, ok Pops? Because I might not be winning any awards for the shit I've done, but you aren't winning Dad-of-the-fucking-year anytime soon either." I jut my finger back in his face as my mother hangs her head in the crossfire.

"What the hell are you talking about?" He spits back, "You gonna give me some sad sack story about how this is all my fault? That you have some kind of Daddy issues. Save it." He rolls his eyes hard.

"You can do that, sure," I snarl. "You go ahead and stand there like you've got any room to look down your nose at me, but you know that you aren't a good father. Just ask Cameron." I bite back. "You think a good father only shows love and respect to their kid if they follow the path they want? You think a good dad is only there for their kids when they're succeeding? You don't care about me, you never did. Cameron used to joke that I was the golden boy, and what a joke it was. I was the golden boy alright, as long as I lived my life to make you happy. You wanna laugh and say I've got 'Daddy issues'? You're right, I do. Because I never grew up with a real father, I grew up with a tyrant who just wanted me to live out your failed dreams."

My father's face is absorbed by crimson and he balls up his fist, "You tryin' to say I'm the failure here?"

"Yeah, you are. You failed at living your big, wild, military dreams and then you failed at being a dad. I guess I learned from the best."

"Hey! Hey! What's going on here?" A staff member enters the room and races over to us. My father and I don't move. We're frozen in rage, staring each other down.

"If you two can't be civil and sit down, we might need to end this visit," the man with wire-rimmed glasses and a comb-over informs us.

"No need to end it, we were already done," Dad doesn't blink or unlock his eyes from mine. "Let's go, Bev. We're leaving."

"Don, please. Can't you just sit down and talk this out. We came all this way," Mom protests weakly.

"I said, we're leaving!" Dad roars.

Mom stands up and runs her hands over her dress pants, pulls her purse on her shoulder and forces herself to hold her head up.

I don't watch as my father storms out of the room. He doesn't deserve any more of my attention. Instead, I look at my mother. I hate that she's crying. I hate that, after everything, I'm still causing her more pain.

"I love you, Jake," she whispers and gives me a hug.

"I love you too, Mom."

"He'll come around. I know he will," she tries to reassure me.

"Sure." I answer, giving her a quick squeeze. Mom follows my father out into the hall and out of the building.

"No he won't," I mutter to myself. "He'll never change."

CHAPTER 18

Holly

I try not to watch how happy the other patients are with their families as I make my way down the hall to my room. The smiles. The hugs. The love. Did my family ever have those moments? I know we did. Back before we fell apart, with a hole torn into our hearts that would never heal. Back before Heather died.

I fight to keep the tears locked up inside, threatening to spill from my broken soul. I'm tired of feeling this way. This guilt. I want to let it go. I need to let it go.

Then do it.

The thought flits through my mind like a butterfly flickering in and out of a warm summer sky. Mesmerizing and beautiful.

I stop in front of the door to my room and lay my hand on the handle. No. I let my fingers slide off the door knob and my arm falls to my side. I'm not going to go wallow in self-pity anymore. I'm not going to hide from the things upsetting me. My parents didn't show up, and yeah, that sucks, but it doesn't mean I'm dead. It's time to stop letting other people control my feelings, letting them control my life.

My mind flashes to Knox, the man who controlled everything I did for five years. He told me what to eat, what to wear, who I could talk to, when I could talk. The worst part was: I let him. I never tried to escape, even when he started beating me, even when he did worse than that. I told myself it was impossible to get away.

And I was wrong.

I stand straight and push back my shoulders, turning on my heel, I make my way back up the hall. If I could stand up to him and start over, then I can face anything. I'm not hiding anymore. I've already made it through hell and lived to tell the tale. If that didn't break me, nothing can.

I march down past the common room full of patients and their loved ones. This time, when I let my gaze wander over them, I don't feel sad. My time will come. I'm not sure when or how, but I know in my heart that I'll be happy again. This too, shall pass. The Alcoholics Anonymous mantra that we've repeated in here a hundred times, pops into my head.

In the meantime, I need to figure out what to do with myself right now. I look around the facility and all the public spaces are filled up with visitors. I don't want to hide in my room, licking my wounds. However, I don't want to sit down next to any of the families like some kind of creeper either.

Shuffling my feet along the tile floor, I make my way to the mail room. I know I don't have any mail, but it gives me a place to go. That's all I'm looking for right now.

"Hey there, I'm Kyle," a short, pudgy man with wiry hair smiles at me. I can't help but stare at his clothes. His sweater looks like one of those joke ones you see people wear to 'ugly sweater parties'.

"Uh, hi," I manage to answer.

"Can I help you with something? I'm sorry, I didn't catch your name," his brown eyes twinkle cheerfully.

"It's Holly, I just… wanted to check on my mail." I finally pry my eyes from the clash of colors and patterns on his body.

"Like the sweater, huh?" Kyle answers.

"Isn't it for Christmas?" I blurt out.

"No, why do you think that?" His face erupts into a smile and I can't help but feel like he wears this thing just to mess with people.

"It's covered in penguins," I point to the design.

"You can wear penguins any time of year," he pulls down on the hem of his gaudy fashion choice and smoothes his hand over the wrinkles.

"In May? I mean, I guess so. But, it's red and green," I laugh.

"So are flowers," he answers with a straight face. Now I'm starting to wonder if he really does think this is a year-round sweater and I'm offending him.

"I guess you've got me there," I smile. "I like it," I lie.

"No you don't," Kyle meets my eyes and I blush. I guess I did offend him after all. "It made you smile though, and that's worth it to me. If I can wear a dorky sweater and make someone's day in here a little brighter, then I don't care how silly it looks," he explains.

"That's really nice," I laugh, relieved that I haven't insulted his tacky taste.

"So, Holly, is it?"

"Yes."

"I need a last name to check your mail."

"Sure, it's Evans," I answer.

Kyle whirls around and searches through one of many filing cabinets lining the back wall. "Evans, ok, just a sec," he runs his hand over the drawers until he reaches the one for names starting with E. I watch as he flips his nubby fingers through the folders in the drawer until he almost reaches the back. "Evans!" He sounds excited as he pulls out a couple of envelopes, "Holly Evans. Here we go, you've got mail today."

"I do," I peer curiously over to the mystery letters in his hand.

"You sure do, now I just need you to sign this sheet," he pulls a clipboard from the top of the filing cabinet with a pen attached to it by a string, "to mark that you've gotten them."

"Sure," I sign the paper and slide it back to him. Wrapping my fingers around the edge of the letters, I tingle with excitement. I can't remember the last time I got mail. I don't mean in here, I mean in life. I forgot the little rush you get when something unexpected is sent to you.

"Thanks!" I cheerfully call out as I start back down the hall to my room. At least this time I'm not going to drown in sadness.

"No problem, and Holly?" Kyle calls out and I turn back to look at him in his ridiculous Christmas sweater once more.

"Yeah?"

"Keep on smiling," he answers.

"I'll try," I beam at him and then hurry back to my room.

I peer down at the envelopes, one of them is clearly from my father. The return address on it makes it easy to figure out. The other is more mysterious. The address to send it here has been printed on a sticker and stuck to the front and there's no return address to be found.

I rush into my room and close the door with my foot, quickly making my way over to my small bed. My fingers make quick work of tearing the edge of the first envelope open and my heart beats quickly as I pull the handwritten letter from my father out.

Dear Holly,

I hope this finds you well. It's been so hard to have you suddenly appear back in our lives only to have you disappear into rehab for two months. I understand that it's important for your recovery, and that's all that truly matters. I know that in time, when you're clean and back home, the communication you aren't allowed to have with us now will fade into a distant memory. It's just hard right now.

I'm writing this because I needed to tell you that we received a notice from Edgewood inviting us to Family Day. Unfortunately, it came really late in the mail and we weren't able to book travel out of the country with such short notice. It kills me to know we could have had time together, and I hope you understand that I would've come if I could.

I'm rooting for you, Holly. I know you're going to get the help you need and live the life you've always deserved; one filled with joy and success. I love you and will be there for your graduation day.

Sincerely,

Dad

I pull the letter to my chest as tears fall down my face. For once, they aren't tears of sadness or fear, but happiness. They didn't just decide not to show up after all. Well, at least my father didn't. I scan his words again, but notice there's no mention of my Mom. I won't focus on that, though. Not right now. Right now, I'll take the small victories where I can get them. Knowing that my father didn't choose to leave me here high and dry on Family Day is feeling like a pretty big win.

I wipe away my tears and put his letter down on my bedside table, smiling. I stare at it in a happy haze as my fingers tear through the next envelope. Maybe things are really going to turn around for me. Once I get out of here, maybe I can get a fresh start. My future feels bright for the first time in over half a decade.

I glance down at the typed letter trembling in my hand. The smile evaporates from my face and my eyes grow wide. I drop the paper to the floor and clamp both of my hands over the silent scream formed on my lips. All the feelings and flames of hope are extinguished by a tide of fear gripping at my heart.

I was so wrong. I have no future. If this is true, I won't

even have a present. I look down at the note in horror. Simply typed, in the middle of the sheet are two lines:

I told you I would find you.
I'm going to kill you.

CHAPTER 19

Jake

I stomp into my room, slamming the door behind me with a clap of thunder. Pacing the empty floor in front of my bed, I try to shake off the anger rolling through my blood.

Who the hell does he think he is? Why did he bother to travel up here from Colorado, just to sit like a sullen lump for our visit?

Rage boils up the back of my throat as his face, tattooed with disappointment, flashes through my mind. I hammer my fists down onto my desk with a thud, but the anger is still there. "Fuck him," I growl at my empty room.

This must be what Cameron has felt like his entire life. The only time my father treated him right was when he spent some time in the Army. As soon as he retired to pursue his dream of a football career, my father's pride shrivelled up into dust. Dad retired as a General, nothing to sneeze at. You'd think his own accomplishments would be enough for him. However, he's never been happy unless his sons were following his path, more like marching down it, in uniform. Even being in the military wasn't really ever enough for him, he always wanted me to be Special Forces, pushing it hard. I'm guessing he wanted to live the adventures he never had in the regular force through me. Too bad my cocaine addiction didn't fit into his 'choose-your-own-adventure' model.

Looking out my window at the lush, green forest surrounding my side of the building I finally feel a calm begin to soothe me. He'll get over it. That much is true. As long as I clean up and stay with the SEALs, that's all he'll need to move on. The night I ran from the cops and left my brother with a bag of coke was a black eye. Not just for my father, but for my relationship with Cameron too. Black eyes heal though. If my brother could forgive me, then Dad will eventually too.

The sliver of good news that my mother delivered pops up from my memory. My big bro got drafted by the NFL! I always knew he'd make it. I can't wait to get out of here and go watch one of his games. Just goes to show that following Dad's dreams aren't worth shit. Cameron broke free, did his own thing and now look at him.

Pride for my brother swells up in my chest and a smile spreads over my lips. I wish I could call him and congratulate him.

THUNK!

My fists ball up at my sides as I whirl around to see who's coming into my room with the grace of a rhino. The tension eases from my body and my fingers unfurl as my eyes lock on Holly's impossible sexiness.

Wait, her eyes, they look glassy. Her face is drained of the usual bright glow I've looked forward to seeing every day. She looks like a corpse, standing in my doorframe with one fist balled up in front of her and her muscles motionless.

"What's wrong? I thought you didn't want us visiting each other's rooms anymore?" I look over her shoulder, out into the hall for possible staff members. Holly doesn't move. It's hard to tell if she's even breathing. I rush over to her and ease her inside my room, gently closing the door behind her.

"What's going on?" I prod. "Holly, please tell me. What happened?" My mind begins to race through worst case scenarios as she stares blankly ahead.

"He found me." Her pale lips barely move as she finally whispers a clue.

"Who found you? What do you mean?" I look down at the fist she's still holding out in front of her, frozen in time. Between the cracks in her fingers I can see she's holding something. A paper.

I softly place my hand on her shoulder, "Holly, it's going to be ok. Let me help you, please." I slide my hand down to hers and she releases the crumpled paper into my hand.

I pull it open and read the typewritten note, if you can call it that.

I told you I would find you.

I'm going to kill you.

A chill runs through me. Knox. He tracked her down.

"Come here, it's going to be ok," I pull Holly against my chest and wrap my arms around her tightly. Her rigid muscles begin to slacken and she falls against me, sobbing. Her tears are wetting my shirt, spreading over my chest like a dark stain. Just like the dark stain from Holly's past haunting her now.

"Shhh, it's going to be ok. I promise you. Don't cry," I run my hand over her silky hair and try to figure out how this piece of shit found her.

"It w-won't be," she sniffles and throws her arms around me tight, pressing her face into me. "He f-found me here. Here! In Canada," she sobs. "He's gonna kill me, he's killed other people who fucked him over, I'm dead."

"Hey, he won't come up here. There's no way he can cross the border, he's just trying to scare you."

"N-no, you don't understand. He wants revenge. He'll find a way. How did he find out I was here?" She wails and I pull her in tight.

"Look, I don't know how he tracked you down here, but he has no reason to try to get revenge. For what? You leaving?" I try to reason with her.

"It's more than that." She pulls her face from my chest and looks at me with her red-rimmed eyes.

"What do you mean?" I hold her loosely in my arms and watch as she seems to debate telling me something, her face twists up like it's painful to think about.

"I shot him," she whispers, dropping her head.

"Wait, what?" Maybe Holly isn't the innocent girl who was stuck in a bad life, like I thought. "Did you say you shot him?"

"I did. In the knee. And I stole his car. And ten grand of his money." She mumbles.

Woah, who the fuck is this chick? Not the woman I've been getting to know in here for the last month.

"Why?" I try to put the puzzle pieces together.

"It's not like I just woke up one day and did it," she looks back up at me and her lip quivers violently. "He was beating me, with a belt…again. Here," she pulls away from me and takes a step back. "See?" she leans over, pulling up her pant leg and prying her sock over her heel. Wrapped around her ankle is the faded yellowing stain of an old, thick bruise. Etched into the side of her ankle is a vague imprint of where that sack of shit hit her with the buckle. My muscles tense as my emotions surge through me. If that fucker shows his face around here, I'm going to fucking end him.

Holly fixes her clothes and stands back up, facing me. "He told me, when he was finished whipping me, he was going to fuck me with his gun," she shivers as she recalls the horror.

"Hey, come here," I reach out and grab her, pulling her back against my chest. "I'm sorry you ever went through that. Any of that. It's over now. You don't need to be afraid."

"Yes, I do!" Her pitch hurts my ears. "He found me! He's going to kill me. He's gonna… "

"No, he won't. Listen, he can't cross the border," I try to explain.

"He has people who can," she protests.

"Ok, even if he does. Even if they try to come here, you're safe here. No one is allowed in this building without a code. You're in a building with twenty-four hour security, in another country, on a property with a fence surrounding it, and you have a secret weapon."

"What?" She scrunches her nose up in confusion.

"Me."

Finally, a smile touches her lips and I can't help but smile back. I want her to feel better. To make her safe. And I'll do whatever it takes to make that happen.

I watch as a cloud rolls in over her bright blue eyes, "What about after I get out? He'll just find me again. At my parents' house!" The revelation strikes her like lightening.

"No. He won't." I assure her firmly.

"How do you know?"

"Does he know where you're from? Where your parents live?" I prod.

"No," she bites her lip and her eyebrows twitch together. "When I left my parents' house, I didn't look back. I never told anyone where I was from, I hoped that if I kept it inside, maybe I would forget too," she looks down at the floor, her chin trembling.

"Ok, and he won't find you there."

"What do you mean? If he found me here, he can find me anywhere."

"He won't find you there, because after this you're going to come live with me. I'll protect you. And if he tries anything when you're living at my house, I'll kill that coward with my bare hands." I pull Holly in close and kiss her forehead.

"Why would you do that for me?" She whispers like she's not sure she wants to know.

"Because," I take a deep breath and look straight into her eyes, "yeah, so um… I'm kind of falling in love with you."

CHAPTER 20

Jake

I can't sleep. I'm tired enough. Bored enough. Yet, every time I close my eyes, nothing. Just more seconds turning into minutes, dragging into hours. I feel like a damned kid waiting up to hear Santa on the roof. In less than ten hours, Holly and I will be walking out of this place. We'll be graduates of the program, free to go back to our lives. Lives we left behind, like shattered tile on the ground. Lives that we'll forge together, as a couple, and create a new picture of our future with the mosaic we build back up.

I twist in the ridiculously small, single bed that I'll never miss sleeping in. Flipping my pillow, I lie my head on the cool side and try, yet again, to let sleep wash over me. My eyes gently shut and I listen to the soft rain pattering on my window pane.

Nothing.

Wide awake. Ok, enough is enough. I'm getting up. I know better than to go prowling into the night in search of Holly's room. We made a promise to each other to hold off from anymore of that until after graduation. I glance at the clock on my nightstand. In nine and a half hours. I groan as I imagine feeling her soft flesh under mine as I fill every inch of her pussy with my hard cock.

Nine hours and twenty-eight minutes.

This is going to be the longest day of my life.

I toss on a t-shirt and jeans then slip into my shoes before heading out. I can't just lie here and miserably wait for time to pass. Besides, there's only so many times a guy can jerk off in one night before he needs to find a different distraction.

My stomach growls at me, directing my feet to the cafeteria. I know the kitchen is closed at this hour, but they keep the drinks and usually some packages of crackers out to subdue late night munchies. Maybe some crackers and a big glass of milk will do the trick. Isn't milk supposed to make you tired or something? I think I heard that somewhere.

I turn the corner and stop dead in my tracks. I guess I did fall asleep. This must be a dream. Across the darkened room, in a light linen gown is Holly. The light of the soda machine glows around her head like a halo. Walking up to her, I notice that this feels more real than any dream I've ever had. The details that are usually blurry around the edges are now crisp.

As I approach, Holly hears my footsteps and whips around, frightened. "Hey, sorry, I wasn't trying to sneak up on ya," I tell her softly, closing the distance between us.

"Oh," her blue eyes look so vibrant under the eerie light casting off the drink machine. "Jake," she breathes, her face relaxing, "it's you."

"It is," I nestle up next to her. "What's a pretty girl like you doing in a place like this?" I tease her, pressing myself against her.

"You're such a dork," she smirks up at me, but the way she presses her pussy against my growing cock tells me a different story. "I couldn't sleep, so I thought I'd get a drink of milk."

I knew I'd heard it somewhere.

Under her nightgown, I can see her nipples form into hard peaks. She looks up at me with her eyes half-closed like she's waiting for me to kiss her. I glance up toward the kitchen door, no one is there. I wind my fingers up in her hair, grabbing a fistful and hover for just a moment over her, breathing her in. This is no dream, this sexy woman, standing in barely anything, this woman I've been dying to fuck since the day we met, is very real.

"Mmmm," Holly moans, testing my restraint. I cover her mouth with my hungry kiss, my tongue easing her lips open and dancing with hers.

I slide both my hands down over her back, cupping her sweet ass and pressing her pussy tight against me. I can't fucking take this. To hell with nine more hours. To hell with one more second. I wrap my hands around each of her thighs and easily lift her up, spreading her legs around me.

Her natural perfume teases my nose and pushes me over the edge. I need her. NOW!

Walking her over to a table, I plop her down on the edge and slide my fingertips under the edge of her nightgown, exposing her neatly-trimmed pussy. "You keeping that trimmed up for me, Holly," I look into her eyes as I run my finger over the short hair.

"Mmmhmmm," she bites her lip.

"Good girl," I mumble as I start to slide down to my knees.

"No, we can't," Holly pulls on my shoulders to stop me.

"Why? It's our last day. Who cares what happens? It's not like they're gonna kick us out on grad day," I fall to my knees and lick my lips, ready to worship her.

"I care," she pleads weakly. I look up at her. Her mouth is telling me a different story than her sexy body, but I still need to listen.

"You're telling me you don't want me to make you feel like you did that night?" I cock an eyebrow at her in disbelief.

"I do," she squirms on the table and my mouth waters. "I really do," she pants. "It's just," she closes her eyes and takes a deep breath. "I made a promise to take this seriously. I want to finish the program by keeping our promise to ourselves and to each other. We said we'd wait. It's only a few more hours. It's important to me," she opens her eyes and stares down at me like she's uncertain how I'll react.

I hate how she looks nervous when she tells me something that she knows I won't like. As if she's expecting me to freak out at her, or worse. Of course, after what she went through with Knox for five years, it's probably a hard habit to break. Still, I want her to trust me.

"Ok," I stand back up and pull down her nightgown. "If it's important to you, it's important to me too. We'll wait," I pull her down from the side of the table to her feet and into my arms.

"Thank you," she presses the side of her face into my chest and listens to my heartbeat. "I love you," she whispers, wrapping her small arms around my waist.

"You don't need to thank me. Never for that. And, I love you too," I smile down at her and give her a quick peck before releasing her to the night. "However, I should go. I'm gonna go take a shower," I smirk.

"Ok, I feel like I should apologize or something," she tilts her head.

"Never." My answer is firm. "Just know, that in nine hours," I growl, "that pussy is mine."

Holly's eyes open wide and she nods her head.

"Good. Well then, sleep well." I grab her hand and give it a squeeze before turning and walking out the door.

Looks like I'll be working on a world record for how many times a guy can jerk off in one night. Damn she makes me crazy, but she's worth the wait. I know that once we get out of here, I'll be working on a new world record. Seeing how many times and how many ways I can fuck her before we're both too sore and tired to continue. Now, that's a record I look forward to setting.

CHAPTER 21
Holly

Standing nervously at the side of the auditorium, I wait to hear my name. I watch as patients who started the program at the same time as me are called on stage, one-by-one, to officially graduate. A little more than fifty percent of us made it through the two months here. Many people quit, choosing whatever their old lives and old addictions provided for them instead of recovery. I knew I had nothing to go back to out there. For me, it was get better or die. "Holly E." Ms. Morehouse calls me up. Even on grad day, they don't reveal our last names. Some attempt to give us anonymity I guess.

I walk up the couple of steps to the center of the stage and shake the hand of the smiling director.

"Congratulations," she speaks softly and hands me a bronze coin with an eagle soaring above the cedars on the front. I flip it over in my hand, the back reads: they who succeed, believe they will.

I smile with tears in my eyes. "Thank you," I whisper.

"You did the hard work, we just helped you find yourself again. Make sure you don't lose her out there, ok?" She gives me a quick hug and I nod, overcome with emotions.

"I won't," I promise and make my way to the other side.

I squeeze the coin in my hand and look out into the crowd of friends and family cheering us on. My eyes stop scanning when they reach the aging face of my father. His cheeks are flush and his smile looks like it hurts, it's so wide. His pride radiates around him like an aura. My heart swells up like a balloon.

I did it.

I've never graduated anything before. Not unless you count kindergarten, which I don't. I dropped out of high school and never looked back. This is the first thing I've really worked for and accomplished in a long, long time. I've been locked in Knox's world of drugs and pain for so long, I'd forgotten what it felt like to achieve something on my own. I fail to recall what it feels like to succeed at anything.

My gaze moves over to my mother. Her face is in direct contrast to Dad's. They look like those masks you always see as a symbol for drama. One with a delirious smile and the other with a frown. Why did she come here? Clearly, she didn't want to.

"Jake A." I pry my attention from the sour look on Mom's face and watch as Jake struts across the stage. I can't help but soak up every inch of him, starting with his shaggy brown hair and ocean blue eyes and traveling down over his broad shoulders, further to his cut abs, to his… I bite my lip and my heartbeat quickens. I remember how I couldn't fully wrap my fingers around his long, fat cock. Heat burns over my cheeks as my chest rises and falls rapidly, only a few short hours and I'll get to explore every inch.

Jake smiles at me as he makes his way to our side of the stage. We did it! My body tingles with a sensation I don't remember having since I was a child: pride. I'm happy that Jake and I agreed to wait until after this ceremony to be together. It meant a lot to me, after years of breaking promises to myself to quit drugs, to leave Knox, to start over, and failing myself every time, this promise had to stick.

Jake looks out at the crowd of strangers, searching. I know what he's going through, I understand what if feels like to scan unfamiliar faces for your family when they aren't there. His eyes stop flickering over the crowd and he juts out his jaw, lined with a much scruffier beard than when we first met. I know he's disappointed that his parents didn't show up today, even if he won't say it.

"And huge congratulations to our graduates of the program. Please, let's give them a hand," the crowd erupts with applause as everyone scatters in different directions, bee-lining for their families.

My father looks like he's competing for speed walking champion as he hurries over to me, my mother slowly wades through the wake of people behind him.

"Holly!" He throws his arms around me in a bear hug. Dad steps back and looks down at me, beaming, "I'm so proud of you honey. I can't wait to get you home and be together as a family again," he smiles.

Mom finally makes her way to his side and scowls at Jake. "Who's he?" She asks rudely.

"Mom, Dad, this is Jake."

"Pleasure to meet you," Jake shakes my father's hand, but my mother crosses her arms tight across her chest and purses her lips.

"Likewise," Dad answers, looking at me with question marks in his eyes.

"Guys, we need to talk. Let's go to my room, I've got all my bags there anyway," I lead the way.

"I told you!" I hear my mother hiss to my father as I guide them from the auditorium with Jake by my side. "She's up to something again," she whispers loudly.

I pretend not to hear her and lead the way to my room. On the floor are my suitcases, already packed and ready to go. My bed is stripped and the drawers and closet have been emptied, prepared for the next lost soul who needs this space.

"So, this is where you stayed, huh?" Dad looks around the small space.

"Yep, this was home for two months," I smile weakly.

"Let's cut the chit chat. Why is he here?" My mother interrupts, her eyebrows knit together and her lips turn down. "What's going on?"

I look up at Jake and he nods at me, "Ok, Mom, Dad, I can't go back with you today. I'm going to need to stay with Jake for a while."

"You've got to me kidding me," my mother's voice is dry as chalk dust.

"No! There's no way you're going with him!" My father protests, puffing out his chest. "Who the hell is this guy? Your boyfriend? It's not happening, Holly. Not again."

"You were supposed to come here to get off drugs, not replace one addicted loser with another one," Mom snaps and throws her arms across her chest like she's trying to touch her hands behind her back.

"Woah," Jake steps in, "with all due respect, Ma'am, you don't know what you're talking about." He holds up his hands.

"Excuse me, but I think we know our daughter better than you. How long have you been in here? A couple of months? Are you going to tell us you're in love next?" Mom rolls her eyes hard.

"Louise, let them talk, please. This isn't helping," Dad interrupts and my mother clamps her mouth shut, billowing out her cheeks like a puffer fish, as crimson rises up her neck.

"Dad," I look into my father's wounded gaze, "please, listen. My ex, the guy I already told you about, he's going to kill me. He found me here, and he'll kill me, and probably you guys if I go back with you." I pull the crumpled sheet Knox sent me from my jeans and thrust it into my father's hand.

He looks down at the short message, then back up at me.

"How do you know he sent it to you?" Dad asks.

"I know. He's dangerous, Dad. He's killed people before," I look down at the tile floor as both my parents watch me in horror.

"Then, we'll just call the police," Dad cuts the silence. "You don't have to go to," he looks at Jake, "where do you live?"

"Virginia Beach, sir." Jake answers.

"You don't have to go, what, fourteen hours away from us to be safe. We'll call the cops and that will be that."

"Dad, you don't understand. He's one of the biggest drug smugglers on the entire East Coast. He's got connections, on the street and in the force. The cops won't help."

"Sir, Ma'am, if I may," Jake interrupts. "I know you don't know me from Adam, but I am a Navy SEAL, I live in a gated community where a lot of my neighbors are also SEALs. Holly will be safe with me. I won't let anything bad happen to her, I promise you that."

"Oh, god, this is rich." Mom groans, "Sounds like a bunch of bullshit to me. You're gonna go run off to Virginia Beach with some supposed Navy SEAL bad boy instead of coming home. Doesn't this sound familiar, Don? How many times is she going to do this to us? How many times are we going to keep letting her walk in and out of our lives?" Mom turns around and walks over to my window, staring out of it, motionless.

"Sir, I don't expect that you'd just take me at my word, especially when you're meeting me in here. That's why I've written down this list of contacts. You can confirm with them that I'm who I say I am. Also, here's my military ID," Jake pulls a card from his wallet and thrusts it out to my Dad along with a sheet of names and numbers he pulled from his pocket.

"Trust me, if Holly goes home with you today, her ex will kill her. I will give her a secure home and I'll take care of her. I swear on my life."

"I will call these numbers," Dad looks down at the sheet and then to me. The tears building up in his eyes break my heart.

"I wouldn't expect anything less," Jake answers softly.

"I just have one question before I do," Dad peers into Jake's face, "you say that if she comes home with us, he'll murder her."

"Yes." Jake answers.

"But, what about if she comes home with you? Won't he still track her down?"

"Sir, if he comes for her at my place he won't have the chance to get to her."

"Why is that?" Dad presses him.

"Because I'll kill him."

CHAPTER 22

Jake

"Hey, are you sure you're ok?" I tuck Holly's hair behind her ear as she looks out the plane window to the snow-peaked Rocky Mountains below.

"Hmmm," she pulls her gaze over to my face like she's awaking from a trance.

"You want to talk about what's on your mind?" I wrap my arm around her and pull her toward me, giving the top of her head a kiss.

"I just… I guess I wish things had gone better with my parents, you know? Well, Dad took it about as good as you could expect really, but Mom…" she trails off and her eyes slide back over to the tiny plane window.

"You're doing the right thing," I reassure her. "I can promise you that." I let my arm drop from her shoulders and grab her hand, giving it a squeeze. "What were you going to do when he tracked you down to your parents' place? You guys would've been sitting ducks. Your mother will come around, she's just worried about you."

"She hates me," Holly whispers, but the pain in her voice screams louder than a delicate newborn, desperate for a mother's love.

"No, she doesn't," my voice is firm. "I can read people pretty well, and I could see that she loves you, deeply." With my finger and thumb, I guide her chin around so she's facing me. "She loves you, Holly."

"Do you think so," her chin quivers as she utters her doubt.

"I know so." I look straight into her bright blue eyes and run my thumb over her rosy cheek. "This is the right call, this keeps your parents safe and it keeps you safe. Once your folks come up to visit us and they have a chance to scope out my neighborhood and my place, they'll see that too, ok?" I kiss the tip of her nose and a smile finally spreads over her full lips.

"Ok," she rests her forehead against mine and runs her delicate hand over my grisly beard.

Holly sits up straight and digs her fingers into my wild man scruff, her face lights up with a mischievous smile.

"What?" I try to figure out what's going on in that beautiful mind of hers.

"Well, one thing is for sure," she tilts her head at me.

"What's that?"

"When we get to your place, I'm going to make you trim down this crazy beard," she laughs.

"Oh, is that a fact?" I run my hand over my jaw. "I dunno, I think I might keep it," I tease her, "it's got a personality now, it's kinda like a pet," I don't bother to tell her that I was going to clean it up anyway.

"I don't know about that, but I know that this thing," she gives my beard a playful tug, "will scratch up the inside of my thighs too much and," she drops her voice and looks around quickly, "I don't want whisker burn on my pussy," she bites her lip and looks up at me with a twinkle in her eyes.

She wins.

I adjust in my seat so my growing erection doesn't push painfully against the zipper of my jeans. "I don't know," I lower my voice, "that's only for good girls, and right now you're being pretty naughty. Getting me all worked up on a plane like this," I nod down to my groin and can't help but smile when Holly looks down with her eyes wide, "I might just have to put you over my knee for that."

"I'd like that," she murmurs.

How can she go from being so angelic she practically has her own halo, to such a sexy bad girl in the blink of an eye? Actually, I don't give a shit how she does it, it's hot as hell and that's all that matters.

I lean toward her and pull her into my kiss, exploring her mouth softly with my tongue. I twist my body so my back is a wide barricade from the aisle and let my fingers slide up under her skirt. I jolt with surprise when they brush up against her bare pussy.

"You're not wearing anything under your skirt," I keep my voice low enough that only our ears can hear.

"No, I'm not," she smirks at me.

I place my finger at her opening, surprised by how wet she is for me. "Maybe you are a good girl after all," I growl, pressing my index finger deep inside her. Holly closes her eyes and breathes out loudly. She's soaking wet. I curl my finger up inside her and apply pressure against her g-spot as Holly wriggles in the seat beside me. Pulling my hand back, I slide my finger back out of her tight little pussy and lick her juices from my hand. "You taste like heaven," I murmur.

Holly's hand slowly slinks up my thigh, but I know there's no way she can pull off slipping her hand into my pants with discretion.

"No," I grab her hand and she looks up at me pouting. "Not here," I tell her firmly. "What you're going to do, is go to that bathroom back there," I jerk my head in the direction, "and you're going to wait for me, cause I'm going to go in there and fuck you raw, understand?" I wait for my good girl to answer, but she can't seem to find her words. Instead, Holly nods silently and quickly stands up, as she slides past me into the aisle, she presses her round ass against my face, toying with me.

I force myself not to watch her head back like I instructed her. I force myself to stare straight ahead and count. Somehow, I reach the count of ninety and stand up, adjusting my cock so its thick ridge is less noticeable to the people I pass as I make my way to the rear of the plane.

The door says "Vacant" and I swing it open too eagerly, quickly stepping inside. Holly is already propped up, her ass on the sink, leaving me just enough room in the ridiculously small space to close and lock the door behind me.

"I've been waiting too long for this," I growl, pulling a condom from my wallet, I quickly unzip my pants and pull them and my underwear down to my upper thighs, "and I won't wait another second."

Holly stares down at me, watching as I unroll the condom over every inch of my heavy dick, I can see from her wide eyes that she's nervous and excited. I don't blame her, she's in for a wild ride.

"Get that sweet ass over here," I grab her and pull her to the edge of the sink. Holly tries to steady herself by grabbing my shoulders, but I quickly take both of her ankles and throw it over my shoulder.

"Oh!" Her eyes meet mine and I can see she wants this as much as I do.

"Shhh!" I scold her quietly. "You have to be quiet."

Holly nods her head and I grab the base of my cock and slide it along her slick entrance. My dick twitches with anticipation as I feel the heat of her pussy against me. I know I should take it slow, but all my self-restraint dissolves as I breathe in her desire.

Stepping into her, I wrap one hand around her shoulders and hold her tight as I sink my cock deep inside her in one thrust. Holly opens her mouth to scream, but I clap my hand over her lips, catching her moans in my broad hand. Her tight pussy clenches around me, and I stay still, looking into her eyes, I let her body make room for me. To adjust to a size, she's clearly not used to.

"You ready," I whisper, dropping my hand from her mouth.

Holly nods and I pull back out a little only to sink deeper inside of her, burying the full length of my cock into her core. This time she doesn't make a sound, instead she looks up at the ceiling, her mouth opened in a silent "O".

"Good girl," I pump my hips against her, faster and harder now. My balls hit against her asshole as I fuck her relentlessly. Her shoulders are tight under my grasp, her leg feels smooth against my shoulder, but I can't pay attention to any of that. I don't even care that Holly is starting to pant so loudly I'm sure it can be heard outside the bathroom walls. All I care about is fucking her sweet little pussy, making up for the lost time, the close calls, the endless nights of fantasies I've had to deal with for the past two months. I'm sure there's a part of her that wanted our first time to be rose petals and candles, but I can't stop myself from holding her tight against me as I thrust my cock inside her like a jackhammer.

I reach down between us and let my finger find her clit, swirling it rhythmically as I pound my cock into her. Holly arches her back and clamps her own mouth with both her hands as I bring her to her orgasm.

Her already tight pussy squeezes down on my cock, driving me to the edge of reason. I can't take anymore; my balls tighten and my cock jerks inside her as the pulsing bliss rips through me and I fill the condom with cum.

I hold her, my cock still inside her and we pant together.

"That was incredible," I whisper in her ear and grab the ring of the condom, pulling out of her. I kiss her lips, gently this time and enjoy the peace that washes over me.

"I love you," she barely breathes the words.

"I love you too," I answer.

"I should go back to the seat," she shakes her head, like she's just realized where she is.

I nod and help her maneuver around me. She slips out the door and I finish cleaning up. Walking back down the aisle, I'm sure I can feel eyes on me. Knowing smiles from strangers. I ignore them. I don't care about what they think. I don't care if the flight attendants heard us. None of it matters.

The only thing that I care about is her. I look at Holly's beaming smile as I reach our seats. If I have her, I don't need anything else in this world, and I'll still have everything.

CHAPTER 23

Jake

My fingers are laced between Holly's as we make our way down the large stairway at Norfolk International. How many times have I flown back here? Usually after a deployment in a country so dirty, destitute and desperate that I've had to fight the urge to drop to my knees in this airport and kiss the ground under my feet with gratitude.

Almost every time I've flown back, it's felt like a huge homecoming, this time is no different. Sure, Canada is a nice country and rehab is definitely not comparable to deployment, but it doesn't change the fact that it feels great to be home.

I look down past the crowd of people in front of us and burst out into laughter.

"What?" Holly tries to follow my gaze with a puzzled look on her face.

Standing at the bottom, off to the side is my brother

Cameron and his lady. Chelsea is holding a sign over her head that says my name, but it's Cameron's sign that has me laughing: "Don't run!" It says on top, then beneath that, "I'm your ride."

Leave it to my big bro to bust my balls after not seeing me for months. He's got a huge grin on his face as I guide Holly over to them.

"I got your message," I laugh. "You got me," I hook my hand with my brother's and pull him into a one-armed hug.

"Good, I didn't want to have to chase you down," Cameron teases me. It's good that we can joke about the night that the cops showed up and I ran off, leaving him with a baggie of my cocaine in his car. At the time, it was the worst night of my life. Probably his too. It feels like a lifetime ago that I was the guy who made that cowardly decision. I can't even relate to that guy now.

"Look at you," I step back from my brother and glance at his fiancée's growing baby bump. "You look radiant," a smile spreads over her face.

"I don't know about that, but I'll take it," Chelsea laughs.

"Holly, this is my big brother, Cameron." I put my arm around her and make the introductions.

"Pleasure to meet you," Cameron shakes her hand and cocks one eyebrow at me, loaded with silent questions.

"And this woman, who you can see is clearly out of his league, is his fiancée, Chelsea," I tease him.

Cameron gently digs his elbow into my ribs, "Hey, I'm trying to keep that under wraps until the wedding is final," he smiles.

"It's so great to meet you both," Holly smiles shyly, tucking her long hair behind her ear.

"Jake, you didn't tell me you found someone. Where have you been hiding this beautiful woman?" My brother nods at Holly.

"In rehab," I answer.

"Oh, are you from Virginia Beach too?" Chelsea asks, not knowing the weight of her question.

"No, I'm from Miami. Well, originally I'm from Everglades City, but I spent the last five years in Miami."

"Really? That's where we're going! Cameron got drafted by the Dolphins, so we're doing the cross-country trek right now," Chelsea answers. She really is glowing. I mean, I know that's a nice thing you're supposed to say to pregnant ladies, but in her case, her caramel skin is shimmering. Pregnancy suits her. It's crazy to think in only a few more months I'm going to be an uncle. It's crazier still to think Cameron will be a father.

"Yeah, Holly needed to get a clean break from Miami, so I offered up my place. Besides, I would miss her too much if she was all the way down there," I wrap my arm around her tight.

"We don't need to get into all of that right now," she squirms in my arm. "We should probably get our bags," she changes the subject clumsily.

"Uh, yeah, they might be out now," Cameron agrees and we all walk over to the baggage claim.

"How did you guys know I'd be flying in now?" I walk beside Cameron.

"Mom told me. She wanted to go to your graduation, but Dad was being… well, you know how he gets." Cameron rolls his eyes.

"Yeah, I do. I mean, you'd know better than I do."

"True, so take it from a seasoned pro, he'll get over himself. You'll go back to being the golden boy in no time," he teases me.

"Whatever," I try to shrug it off. I don't want to care about what my father thinks. There's a small, nagging voice in the back of my brain that keeps telling me differently though.

The girls are chatting behind us and giggling. It's nice to see Holly hit it off with someone. My brother rests his hand on my shoulder and looks me straight in the eyes, "Hey, man, don't worry about him. Ok? Besides, I know you probably didn't really care much about the whole rehab thing, but I'm proud of you for doing it," he claps my shoulder.

"No, it did mean something to me. I mean, not at first. I thought the whole thing was a dumb joke, you know?" Cameron nods his head at me. He gets it, I'm sure he's seen his fair share of people being shipped off to addiction facilities just to clear their name, and not their heads. "But, we had a Canadian soldier come in and speak about addiction and all that, and something clicked. I realize that I had a problem. I needed to be there." I confess.

Cameron's eyebrows raise and he looks over my face like he's waiting for me to throw out a punchline. He smiles brightly at me, "That's awesome, man. I'm glad it helped ya."

We gather around the rotating conveyor of luggage and wait. Duffle bags and suitcases belonging to strangers whirl around and I keep my eye out for mine.

"Oh, there's my suitcase," Holly tries to reach her peach bag, but it's toward the inside and her hand can't grasp it. I lean over and easily pluck it from the cluttered baggage claim and plop it down on its wheels.

"Thanks," she stands up on her tiptoes and gives me a quick peck.

"Aww," Chelsea smiles at us. "You two are so cute together. Aren't they, Cameron?"

"Oh yeah, adorable," my brother answers, his voice dead-pan. I can't help but crack a smile. It's great to see him again, to know that we're still good after everything that happened.

"Did you ask him yet?" Chelsea looks back and forth from my face to my brother's with her deep, brown eyes.

"Ask me what?" I look at Cameron.

"I was gonna let him grab his suitcase first, Miss Impatient," he softly scolds her.

"Good timing," I pluck my bag from the conveyor and place it next to my feet. "So, what's up?"

Cameron smiles at Chelsea and then looks to me, "Ok, so, I didn't just come here to give you a drive home."

"Oh no?"

"I also wanted to let you know that Chelsea and I are going to get settled in Miami and then, we're getting married."

"Really? That's awesome! Wow, that's gonna be busy, isn't it?"

"Yeah," Cameron answers, "it's going to be a whirlwind, for sure. But, we wanted to get married before the baby, it's important to Chelsea, so it's important to me," he lifts his fiancée's brown hand and kisses it. "And with training camp starting up in July, we wanted to have the ceremony before all that craziness begins," he explains.

"That's great! You're having it in Miami then?"

"Yep, we figured, since it's just family going, it would be a nice way to show them our new place and all that too."

"Makes sense," I smile down at Holly, but her eyebrows are knit together with worry.

"Anyway, sorry for springing this on you, but I'd love if you'd be my best man, Jake. I can't think of anyone else who could even come close to filling those shoes."

"Aww, man," I throw my arms around him and give his back a clap, "of course I will. It would be my honor," I answer truthfully. "When is the wedding?"

"In two weeks, I know it's short notice," he holds up his hands, "but I wanted to ask you in person, you know?"

"Yeah, no problem. I understand. I'll be there," I grab my suitcase and Holly and I follow Chelsea and Cameron toward the exit.

"Miami? In two weeks?" Holly whispers. "I can't go. I won't be safe. What about Knox?"

Oh shit, I forgot about that.

CHAPTER 24

Holly

"Wow, that was amazing," Cameron pushes his empty plate forward on the table and slumps back into his seat.

"Don't tell my mother, but that was the best roast I've ever eaten," Chelsea smiles at me warmly.

"Thank you, it was nothing, really," I stand up and begin to clear the table.

"Here, let me help you with that," Chelsea grabs some dirty dishes and brings them over to the sink with me.

"They're right, that meal was delicious," Jake turns in his chair to talk to me. "I don't know what I did to get so lucky, but you're the whole package. Beautiful, smart, a great cook."

"Aww," Chelsea looks from Jake's face to mine, glowing with happiness.

"Yeah, wait till she gets a taste of your cooking," Cameron makes air quotes with his fingers and sticks out his tongue like he has a rotten taste in his mouth.

"What are you talking about? I'm a great cook," Jake puffs out his chest.

"Oh yeah, if you ever get a craving for gross boxed food, this guy is your man," Cameron juts his thumb toward his brother.

"Oh, I know you're not slamming my signature dish right now. Frank's Alive is awesome and you know it. You're just jealous you didn't invent it." Jake smirks.

"What on earth is 'Frank's Alive'?" I head back over to the table and the guys stand up and start gathering the cutlery and glasses.

"Only a culinary masterpiece," Jake jokes.

"You poor girl, it's only a matter of time until he whips it up for you." Cameron carries the glasses over to the kitchen counter. "Imagine Kraft macaroni and cheese, with hot dogs in it," he explains.

"Oh, I've had it like that before," I shrug.

"No, I'm not done yet, so it's also got probably half a cup of relish in it and a bunch of mustard mixed in."

"What?" Chelsea scrunches up her nose.

"Yeah, Jamie Oliver over here threw it together when we were kids and our mom was horrified. She asked Jake what it was supposed to be, thinking he messed up the easiest food in the world to make and he said…"

"Frank's Alive!" Jake jumps in.

"Why did you call it that?" I look over at him.

"No idea, I was probably nine or so. The name stuck though, and so did the recipe. I'll have to make it for you sometime," he walks up to me and slides his arm over my shoulders.

"Uh, that's ok. I can do the cooking," I smile up at him.

"Smart," Cameron nods at me.

"All right, maybe I'm not a great chef," Jake looks at his brother.

"You can say that again," Cameron answers.

"However, Frank's Alive is delicious. I stand by that meal," Jake pretends to pout.

"I'm sure it is," I rub my hand over his shoulder pretending to soothe his bruised ego.

"Don't worry about the dishes right now, we can just relax or watch a movie if you want," Jake offers.

A movie. The idea almost feels foreign. After sixty days of no television, except for the occasional Alcoholic Anonymous footage, watching a movie almost sounds like a sinful luxury.

"No, we actually gotta hit the road," Cameron answers and Chelsea leans her head against his shoulder tenderly.

"What? You're not going to drive to Miami now are you? It's already seven o'clock. Isn't it like twelve hours away?" Jake protests.

"It's almost fourteen, and we have no choice bro. I've gotta check in with the team by noon tomorrow. I'm going to pull an all-nighter and drive straight through."

"That's not very safe," I interrupt.

"It's no biggie," Cameron waves off my concern. "I'll pull over and catch some winks if we get too tired."

"If you want, you can sleep for the first bit and I'll drive, then we can switch out," Chelsea wraps her arms around Cameron's waist.

"Brains and beauty," Cameron murmurs to her, "I can't wait to marry you," he kisses her quickly.

"Ok, well, give me a call when you get in so I know you made it ok," Jake interrupts the lovebirds' moment.

"Will do," Cameron heads to the back hall of Jake's bungalow with his fiancée.

"It was great to see you again," Jake smiles at Chelsea, "and it was ok seeing you too," he jokes with his brother.

"Yeah, yeah," Cameron smiles and puts on his shoes. "In all seriousness, though," he stands up and claps his hand onto Jake's bulky shoulder, "you've got a great thing going on here, a second chance," the brothers look at each other, "don't fuck it up."

"I won't." Jake nods solemnly.

"I'm proud of you, man," Cameron throws his arms around Jake and the two share a huge bear hug.

"That means a lot to me, Cameron," Jake's voice is soft and full of emotion. "Thanks for asking me to be your best man."

"I wouldn't dream of asking anyone else," Cameron steps back and the two stand a little taller. "Ok, we're off," Cameron clears his throat. "We'll call you when we get there," he opens the door for Chelsea.

"It was great meeting you," I call out.

"You too," Chelsea and Cameron answer as they make their way out the door.

We watch as they get into their car and wave as they pull out of the driveway. "So," Jake closes the door and looks down at me, "it's just you and me now," a smile curls the corners of his lips.

"It sure is," I answer coyly.

"It's nice having you here," Jake runs his thumb down the side of my face and I tilt my head. "There's just one problem with this whole situation."

Problem? I squint my eyes and frown, trying to think of what I could've done, "What's that?" I search his face.

A mischievous twinkle glints in his eye as he smirks at me, "You're wearing entirely too much clothing."

CHAPTER 25

Holly

"Well, that is a pretty serious problem," I laugh.

"I'm afraid we're going to have to do something about that right now," Jake locks the door behind me and suddenly scoops me off my feet.

"Hey! What are you doing?" I fake protest, kicking my feet playfully in the air. Jake effortlessly tosses me over his shoulder and starts walking down the hall.

"I told you, we've gotta fix this issue," he laughs. "There's only one way I want to see you right now," he kicks open his door to the bedroom and struts in.

"How's that?"

"Naked," he tosses me down onto the bed. "Now," he demands.

Kneeling on his bed, I tug my shirt up over my head and toss it to the floor, my heart races as I unhook my bra. I've never seen a man who looked so hungry for me before. The fire in Jake's eyes is as intimidating as it is exciting.

Slowly, I slide the straps down my arms, teasing him.

"That's it," he circles his hands around my waist and flips me back onto the mattress. His fingers quickly unbutton my jeans and he rips them from my legs desperately, pulling off my underwear with them.

"You're so fucking sexy," his voice is gravelly and deep. My nipples peak and I squirm under his gaze. Heat flushes over my entire body, sweeping over me like a wildfire.

Jake's eyes are locked on mine, even as he pulls off his shirt. As soon as it's over his head, he's holding me in place with his intense stare. I lean on my elbows, arching my back and pushing out my breasts.

"Show me how wet you are for me," he demands and I slide my hand down over the curve of my hip to my lower lips. I slip my finger into my folds and hold it out to him, covered in my juices. Jake grabs my hand and licks my finger clean.

"I love how you taste," he murmurs. He hooks his thick arms around my knees and drags me to the end of the bed until my legs are dangling off the side. Dropping to his knees, he drapes my legs over each shoulder and takes a long, slow lick between my legs.

"Mmm," I writhe on the bed, bucking my hips up to meet his tongue.

"That's right, baby. Now you don't have to be quiet. I wanna hear how good I'm making you feel. I'm going to make you scream," he breathes on my pussy and I wiggle under him, desperate to feel his soft tongue once more.

Jake doesn't keep me waiting, he slides his tongue between my lips and flickers it over my clit making me cry out.

"Fuck that feels so good," I moan.

He slides one of his fingers inside me, moving it until he hits a spot that makes me vibrate with pleasure. The feeling is intense, his tongue lashing against my clit and the spot inside me he's pressing, it's almost too much.

Suddenly, I feel another finger slide between my ass cheeks and I wriggle under him nervously. He presses against my asshole, but doesn't push inside. The pressure alone is enough and it heightens the intense pleasure building up within me.

Jake relentlessly chases my orgasm with his tongue until my body can take no more. I squeeze my eyes shut and throw back my head as ecstasy shudders through me in an explosion. I writhe against the sheets, surrendering to my bliss and crying out so loud that my throat is raw.

"Oh Jake!"

"Mmm, that's what I like to hear," he stands up, leaving me limp and panting on the bed as he grabs a condom from his night side table.

"That was amazing," I try to get my breathing under control and watch as Jake flicks open his pants and steps out of them. His cock is huge. I stare at it, mesmerized.

"Don't put it on," I nod at the foil packet between his finger and thumb. "I want to taste you," I kneel at the edge of the bed.

"I'm not going to argue with that," Jake walks over to me and I grab his fat cock with both of my hands. I slide my tongue over the tip and he growls a deep, guttural sound.

Opening my mouth wide, I slip my lips over his girth and try to take him into my mouth. "That's it," he smiles down at me, "you can do it." He gently rests his hand on my head and I try to relax my jaw and slide more of him inside my mouth. I can't fit him all, there's still too much.

I pull back and slide my lips over him again, bobbing my head faster I pump from the base of his cock in sync with my mouth.

"Fuck, that's good." Jake closes his eyes and tangles his fingers up in my long hair, pulling me into him. As I bob my head back toward his sensitive tip, I swirl my tongue over him and he groans loudly while pushing on my head harder. I feel his dick twitch on my tongue and I continue to pump my hands faster, in time with my mouth.

Jake's breathing is ragged and his muscles are rigid as his cock spurts his warm cum inside my mouth. I swallow every last drop, eager to make him feel as good as he made me feel.

"Oh fuck, I really am the fucking luckiest guy. That was amazing," Jake pulls back, freeing himself from my mouth.

"I'm glad," I smile up at him.

He plops down on the bed next to me and pulls me into his arms, wrapping them around me. "I love you, Holly," he murmurs, running his hand over my hair and down my back softly.

"I love you too, Jake." I whisper. Safe in Jake's arms, I snuggle into him and let sleep tug me into another world.

CHAPTER 26

Jake

I pull the trigger and the boy falls to the floor with a thud. His mother's screams pierce my eardrums as a tide of crimson gushes from the child onto the floor. I'm frozen. I can't look away from his lifeless, little body. I can't see him as the enemy. As a terrorist. He's just a boy. Just a boy.

I sit up in bed with a start, gasping for breath and my heart thudding erratically in my ribs. Cold sweat trickles an icy trail down my back. I squeeze my eyes shut and try to fill my head with a different image. I try to push away the same dream that's been haunting me since my deployment.

I open my eyes and my heart slows its beat as I look over at Holly. She looks so innocent, so beautiful, peacefully sleeping beside me.

She already escaped one monster's bed. I can't help but wonder if she's just slid into another's. I know I'll never lay a hand on her. I'll never hurt her in any way. Ever.

But, when your country pins a medal on your chest and tells you you're a fucking hero for ending a child's life, it's hard to feel like anything but a monster.

He had a gun. I repeat the thought like it's my own personal slogan. He would've killed you.

I know it's true. It doesn't matter though. No amount of facts or reasoning will ease the pain in my soul.

With my breathing back to normal, I slip back down under the covers and roll toward Holly, scooping her into my arms. I peer over at the alarm clock. Less than an hour before I've got to get up for work. I can't think of any better way to spend that time than to hold her.

Holly mumbles something incoherent and settles her head down onto my chest, breathing softly. I run my hand over her long hair and trail the tips of my fingers on her creamy skin.

I don't want to leave her here today. The realization hits me like a sucker punch to the gut. For the first time since I joined the SEALs, I'm not excited about going to work. In fact, the twisting ache in my stomach feels a hell of a lot more like dread than anything.

A life without the SEALs was one I never thought I'd want to live. Now, after only two months away, with Holly, it doesn't hold the same luster.

I breathe her scent deep into my lungs like it's the very oxygen I need to stay alive. Wrapping my arms around her tight, I want to freeze this moment in time. This perfect peace that comes with holding the woman of my dreams as she gives me all of her trust, and all of her heart.

You need to release.

I shake my head violently, as if I can toss the intruding thought out of my brain. Where did that come from? I can't release from the military. What would I do with my life? Who would I be?

I lazily draw invisible designs on Holly's skin and try to focus on just this moment. Not my deployment. Not what work will bring. Not retirement. Just now. Because, right now, with Holly in my arms and the problems of the world still locked outside my bedroom walls, this moment is perfection.

CHAPTER 27

Jake

"Hey man! It's good to see your ugly mug around here again," Petty Officer Black nails me in the shoulder as I walk into our mess.

"Thanks, man. It's good to be back," I'm happy it's not a lie. It seems like my nervousness this morning was unfounded. So far, everyone has been incredibly welcoming, almost like the coke incident is water under the bridge and the guys are just happy to have me back.

"Yeah, so you did a couple months at a spin-dry, huh?" Black unlocks his locker and rummages inside.

"Yep, up in Canada. It wasn't too bad actually," I look up at my bunk, it's been stripped clean but at least it hasn't been taken over by some new guy. It's really hard to get the middle rack on a ship. With the bunk beds stacked three cots high, the lowest rack is like sleeping on the floor and the top one is a pain in the ass to get out of if you need to take a piss in the middle of the night. My bed is that perfect, Goldilocks level, that's easy to get in and out of.

"So, what? Did they break you down? Tell you partying is the devil? Bring you to Jesus?" Black looks up at me with a smug smile, rolling his eyes.

"Nah, not exactly man." I'm not going to stand here and try to explain the moments of clarity I felt in rehab to Black. He and I go way back, we've partied together more times than I could even begin to count. Eight balls of coke and hot, nameless chicks in every port was our specialty. I smile as I remember my white, five-nine friend using his standard line on the ladies, "Once you go Black, you'll never go back. By the way, I'm Dan Black." He loved using his name in that old line usually reserved for black guys. The thing was, chicks loved it. They always laughed, which broke the ice and then, putty.

"I knew they wouldn't break you," Black smiles broadly, standing up and stretching his arms wide. "You know, after work me and a couple of the guys are gonna head out for a few drinks. You should come along," he twists his thick arms like he's trying to loosen up his tight muscles, instead of showing off the bulk he's added to his frame since I left.

"I don't think so man, I'm gonna pass," I ignore his peacocking and throw my gear into my old locker, fastening it shut with a padlock.

"What? Come on, it'll be good times. What are you gonna do instead? Go home and jerk off? Come out, it'll be a blast," he stares at me hard.

I don't blink, he's not going to wear me down with his high-pressure sales tactics, "Don't need to jerk off, gotta hot girl waiting for me."

"You?" Black looks at me sideways, "you got a girlfriend?"

I shrug, "Yep."

"Man, you have changed," my old party friend eyes me suspiciously.

"Hey! Armstrong! Black! Get your asses up to the Captain's cabin! There's a debrief going down in less than five minutes and you better be there!" Chief Jackson barks at us from the door, interrupting an already dead conversation.

"Will do!" I yell back, taking my cue to leave. I don't wait for anymore of Black's deep insights, instead I head out to the flats and up the ladder to the deck above. I wheel around the corner into the room just as the PowerPoint presentation hits the screen.

I join my guys along the back wall, behind all the officers crowding the couches and seats in the front.

"All right! Listen up! We've got intel on the situation in Syria and you're going to want to listen. It looks like we're going to be putting boots on the ground in just over a month, so pay attention. This debrief could save all of your lives," Second Lieutenant James walks slowly in front of the small crowd. "Lieutenant Huang, you're up," he directs the intelligence officer to take his place.

An absurdly young looking officer with black hair and black eyes wastes no time hustling to the front of the cabin. He pushes a tiny remote in his hand and pulls up the first slide, a page of facts and figures about the Syrian government's atrocities.

"As you well know, the Bassah regime has been overthrown by the rebels and these figures here, well, they seem downright soft and cuddly compared to the shit going down over there now." Huang clicks his tiny remote and the picture changes to a city in ruins. Buildings blown into dust and rubble, indistinguishable from one another, collapsed into the sand.

I blink hard, trying to stay focused. I don't want to feel the heat of the boiling Middle Eastern sun burning my skin. I don't want to see the permanent sunspots in my eyes. I push them away. Focus. Breathe and focus.

Huang's voice cuts back in as my vision clears, "… unprecedented attacks on civilians, with no regard for casualties, including women and children," he clicks his button and a decimated elementary school appears on the screen. I breathe in sharply as the young bodies of dead children are strewn over the whiteboard.

My hands tremble and my breathing quickens as goosebumps break out over my arms. I see the boy, he has a gun. He points it at me, I don't think, just react. Two shots and he drops. It's only once I see him on the floor that I realize just how small he is. What grade would he be in? Two? The blood pours from his corpse as his mother shrieks a deep, animal-like howl at the pain of losing a child. He had a gun. I had to shoot. He had it pointed at me. It was me or him. I had to take away his future to preserve my present.

Sweat breaks out across my brow and the trembling in my hand quivers through my legs. I feel sick.

"Hey man, you good?" Black suddenly appears in my vision. I look around and the room is clearing out. I missed the brief. How did that happen?

"Yeah, for sure," I lie, looking at the ground.

"Big day for you, huh? First day back and you find out we're back to it next month. Time to go be a fucking hero!" Black claps his hand on my back and my mind flashes to my medal ceremony.

"For bravery and valor," the Captain pinned it to my chest as I winced at the words. "You're a hero, Son."

A hero.

"Yeah, big day," my words are flat. I follow Black out of the cabin dizzily.

"All right, bro. It's almost quitting time. You sure you don't wanna come out after work? It would be good to have a couple of drinks with you again. I've missed you, man." Black pushes me.

"You know what," I pause as the images flash back in my mind. I push them away, "That sounds good. Just a couple of drinks and then I'm out."

"I knew you wouldn't change!" Black smiles broadly and heads down the ladder with me on his heels. "Fuck all that rehab shit, right? You do what you gotta to stay in the SEALs, but fuck it," he exclaims.

"Just a couple though. No other shit. No shots. Ok?" I answer.

"Yeah, yeah. A couple of drinks. For sure. Glad to see you're back, man!" He smirks like he's accomplished something.

"Yeah," I push the last of my nerves and memories down into the pit of my gut, "great to be back," my words taste as gritty as the desert sand on my tongue. "Great to be back."

CHAPTER 28

Holly

I smear the peanut butter on my toast, making sure I push it over to each edge. It feels weird to eat alone after living with Knox, who never let me out of his sight for five years, and then going to Edgewood, where I was surrounded by hundreds of fellow addicts for every meal. I lift the toast to my lips and the crunch is deafening. I need some background noise. Listening to myself chew is depressing.

I grab the remote and flick on the large, flat television suspended on the wall. A crowded table of aging ladies fills the screen as The View comes on. I watch for a second, as they talk over each other, all trying to make their point loudly and at the same time. It sounds like the chaos of the rehab cafeteria. The noise settles my nerves and I grab my food, not really focusing on what they're saying, just enjoying that they're saying it.

Plopping down on the couch, I smile stupidly at the toast on my plate. It probably makes me weird, but getting groceries with Jake a couple of days ago, was a real highlight of the week for me. I'm sure for most people it's a chore, just another thing to check off their weekly to-do list, but I loved the simple luxury of choosing food with my man. Being out, on his arm, doing something as meaningless as picking out apples with him was a real treat.

I never realized how pent up Knox kept me for over five years of my life. We rarely ever left his place, between his job and his cocaine-induced paranoia, he didn't like leaving his apartment much. I was never allowed to go anywhere on my own, and I let that become a normal part of my existence. How? I shake my head. He treated me more like an animal than a person, telling me when I could eat, when I could speak. For years, we lived almost exclusively on food he ordered in. It's amazing I still have my health at all. Not that my cocaine addiction left me much of an appetite anyway.

My body was as hollow and vacant on the outside as my soul was on the inside. So, yeah, maybe I'm a huge dork for loving trips to the grocery store, but it's the little things.

I drop the crusts down onto my plate and brush the crumbs from my top. My thoughts trail off to my parents. I wish they could see how happy I am now. They were so upset about me coming to live here, I hope they take Jake up on his offer to come visit us. I know after only a few hours, they're minds would be put to rest if they saw how peaceful and happy my life is now.

I should give them a call. The idea of listening to my mother's frosty tone squeezes my heart too hard to bring myself to do it. Maybe an e-mail would be better. Before he left Edgewood, my father wrote down all his contact information and stuffed it in my hand. None of it had changed from when I was a kid, the phone number, his 'PapaBear' email address. Hell, he even wrote down their house address, like I hadn't just taken a taxi there a couple of months ago. I guess after I disappeared from their lives, he didn't want to take any chances that I would lose touch with them again.

I walk over to Jake's computer, which he gave me the password to earlier. "Mi casa es su casa," he smiled. "This is your place, eat what you want, do what you want, ok?" He kissed my forehead and I closed my eyes with a smile.

I open my e-mail and can't get in. What the hell? Oh, I forgot that I changed the password before I headed off to rehab so Knox wouldn't be able to access my account anymore. My email was just one more thing that he controlled when I lived with him. I never gave him a reason not to trust me, I was stupidly loyal to that asshole, but he still insisted on checking my messages whenever he was feeling jealous.

I log in properly with the new password and gasp. My inbox is filled with message after message from Knox. I scroll the screen, he sent the first one a couple of days after I left. There must be hundreds of them here! I click them, scanning the messages and my heart sinks. Most of the messages are short and read pretty much the same way, he's going to find me. I can't escape.

I scroll up through the madness and see his tone started to change when he found out I was at Edgewood. That's when he started the death threats. I guess he figured out I wasn't reading his messages and that's why he sent me that letter.

Flicking past a bunch of unopened e-mails I look at the

last one he sent me. It's dated from a week ago. Clicking the message, I see it's more of the same. Another death threat. It seems like he's losing steam though. The messages are spaced further and further apart. That must be a good sign.

I hover my mouse over the little x in the corner, I don't have the heart to get a hold of my parents right now. I think I need to take a long bath and soak of the black stain that Knox has left on me.

Da-ding!

I jump in the leather chair and my eyes grow wide as a new e-mail pops into my inbox. It's from him. My arms feel like a thousand tiny acupuncture needles are prickling my skin as a shiver violently runs down my spine.

Does he know I've been checking my e-mails? Paranoia washes over me, I look around Jake's house, like I expect Knox to walk out from behind the living room curtain or something.

I'm being irrational. It's a coincidence. Nothing more. I take a deep breath, but the icy feeling in my gut doesn't melt away. My hand trembles as I let my curiosity battle with my fear. Finally, I click the message open and jolt upright in the chair, clasping both of my hands over my mouth to contain a scream that rattles in my throat.

I leap to my feet, my heart thrashing in my chest and look at the screen in horror. There, glowing from Jake's computer is a picture of us, standing with a half-filled grocery cart and wide smiles frozen on our faces. We're completely oblivious to our picture being taken, our eyes locked on one another in what would be a sweet picture if it was taken under any other circumstance.

Under the picture, his message is simple. Tears spring

to my eyes and I struggle to breathe. This time, there's no death threat. No detailed plans to shoot my legs or explicit messages about how he plans to fuck me. Instead, only two words are under the photo: Found you.

Fuck. Shit. Fuck!

There's no way Knox was at the grocery store, was there? Is there any possible chance he could've been standing close enough to us to take our photograph, but I didn't see him? No. It's impossible.

The thought brings me no comfort. That means he's got someone else following me. He knows where we are. It's only a matter of time until he comes to collect.

I rush over to the kitchen drawer and pull out the biggest knife I can find, racing down the hall, I lock myself in Jake's room. He could come for me in a week, or a month, or fucking today. The only thing I know for sure is that he will stop at nothing to take me back. To teach me his lessons. To kill me.

I slide under the comforter, shivering like a little girl afraid of the monsters in her closet. It's funny how, when we're kids, we're so afraid of scary creatures lurking under our beds. Crazy concoctions our imaginations come up with that have no basis in reality. No one tells us that the real monsters live among us. That we work with them, we date them, we see them every day.

As long as my monster is out there, lurking in the shadows, I'll never be safe.

He'll never stop, until he destroys me.

CHAPTER 29

Jake

"So, we're standing there, trying not to sway all over the place," Black is leaning into the crowd, loving that they're hanging off his every word. "And were trying to not even breathe too heavily, cause we absolutely reek of liquor," Black's eyes twinkle as he captivates the table full of sailors.

I can't help but smile at how he paints a picture. Black can be a dick, but him and I have history. We ripped it up in every port together. Most of the time, the party didn't stop when we hit home soil either. I can't count the number of drunken, coked out nights we've had. Mostly because I can't remember them.

"And he says to us," he continues, "'I'm only going to ask you one more time, how the fuck did this monkey get on board?'" He drops his voice as he imitates our old Captain. "And this one," he starts to laugh, jutting his thumb at me, "says 'I don't know, sir. Maybe he enlisted.'" The table erupts with laughter as Black doubles over. I can't help but chuckle too, even if I'd rather forget what a shit show I used to be.

"That's fucking epic!" A young recruit with no more than three haircuts in the navy beams at us. He looks at us the way I remember looking at the older guys when I first joined. Like they were rock stars and royalty rolled into one. In my world, there was nothing cooler than the grizzled SEALs who had a bunch of deployments under their belt.

"What happened to the monkey?" Some other guy I only met today asks.

"The Captain tossed him off the ship," Black smirks.

"Really?" His deep brown eyes squint.

"No, he's shitting you. The Singapore government sent some animal control people to take him back before we left port," I explain.

"You always gotta ruin my fun." Black pretends to pout for a second, but he can't keep the wide smile from his face. "Man, we had some wild days, didn't we?"

"We did," I agree. To hear him tell it, you'd think it had just been a non-stop party. Of course, telling stories about late night cocaine confessions and hugging toilet bowls probably wouldn't get the same idolization. Even if we did spend just as much time doing those things as we did messing around and being crazy. Maybe even more.

Dan blazes into another story and I pat my hands over my jacket pockets. Where's my phone? I slide my palms over my pants, but it's not there either. Shit. I must've left it in the car.

I peer around the bar, but there's no clock on any of the walls. Glancing out the window, the sky is already turning a murky cocktail of deep blues. Is it night already? How long have we been here?

"Hey man, sorry to interrupt," I cut off Black, "what time is it?"

"Uh, I dunno," he shrugs and pulls out his cell. "Almost eight, why?"

What? How is that possible? We came in here for a couple of drinks almost four hours ago. How did the day slide into night without me noticing?

"I've gotta get moving," I start to stand up but Black grabs my arm.

"What? No way! It's still early, bro. I haven't seen you in forever, you can't take off yet," he demands.

"No, I've got my girl waiting for me at home. I'm going to head out," I pull my arm back and stand up.

"Oh, come on, she's a big girl. She can look after herself for a few hours while you catch up with old friends, right? Besides," he drops his voice, but everyone at the table can still hear him, "after this I was gonna have you come over. You know, and give our buddy Paul a call." He throws the name of my old dealer out casually.

"No, I'm not interested," I clamp my jaw and look him in the eyes.

"For fuck's sake!" He throws his hands up in the air. "I knew they got to you," he eyes me up with disgust. "You going to be one of those holier-than-thou guys now who tells everyone they party too much? You can't even go out and have a good time anymore? What did they do to you in that place? Shove a stick up your ass?" Black slurs at me.

"Things change, man. People do too." I blow him off

and start to leave.

"Ok, ok. Listen, I'm sorry man. That wasn't cool of me. Hey, lemme buy you a shot, ok? I wanna make it up to you." Black grasps my coat sleeve and I look down into his hopeful face.

"You don't have to do that."

"No, I want to. You know what?" He stands up and waves his hand at the perky bartender across the room, "Hey, sweetheart! How about you grab us a round of Irish Car Bombs. One for everyone, ok?" He circles his finger around the table. "It's on me," he smirks at his happy group of friends.

I look over at the young lady putting together Black's order and then back to the man. "Ok, one shot," I shrug. "Just one and then I've gotta peel out of here, ok?"

"All right! That's the guy I know!" Black claps my shoulders enthusiastically and pulls my chair out for me to sit back down. I plop into it, sinking into the wooden chair and watch as he sits tall next to me, puffing out his chest proudly.

Just one shot, then I'm out. That's it. No wild night with Black, no trolling for cocaine, none of that. Just one shot.

Just one.

CHAPTER 30

Holly

I peer over at the alarm clock on Jake's night table. It's almost eleven. It's pitch black outside and every set of car headlights that passes by the bedroom window, casting ominous light across the walls, grips my gut with fear. Is it Jake?

Or is it Knox?

I know the house is in a gated community, but I also know it won't stop Knox. He's already tracked me down to this city, it's only a matter of time until he zeros in on this house.

Where is Jake? My eyes squeeze shut and I silently pray, again, for him to come home safe. Did Knox follow him? Did he kill him? Did he take him? He was supposed to be home over six hours ago, I've called his phone a hundred times, and have only managed to fill up his voicemail with frantic messages.

Jake is a Navy SEAL, he can take care of himself, I

reassure myself. Except the thought does little to comfort me. Especially when Knox is a stalker with a cold gun in his hand and the heat of revenge burning through him. You can be the most elite combat arms soldier with the most rigorous and specialized training in the world, but it won't save you from being shot in the back of the head. Nausea overwhelms me at the thought of Jake being slumped over his steering wheel, with blood dripping down his face and a hole blown into the back of his skull. I'll never forgive myself if something happens to him.

Of course, the guilt won't have time to consume my flesh like burning flames, because if Knox got to Jake, then my time is ticking down. I'll be dead by morning. Or whenever he's finally done "punishing me".

Headlights pour through the window and wash the bedroom wall with white light. I can hear the rubber tires of a car slowly pull into the driveway. I grip the handle of the knife I pilfered from the kitchen and tiptoe over to the side of the window, peering out through the side of the blinds.

It's not Jake's car. My heart sinks and the lump I've been trying to swallow all day grows even larger in my throat. It's a cab.

Fuck.

I watch in horror as a shadowy shape slides out of the back seat and slams the door shut. Would Knox show up here in a taxi, to kill me? I did steal his car, but I can't imagine him not replacing it. Unless he's trying to keep his attack anonymous from the suburban busy bodies. It's a lot harder to identify a man arriving in the middle of the night in a taxi than in a tricked-out Escalade.

I lunge away from the window and twist my neck as I

search the room for a place to hide. Under the bed? No, I can't use my knife if I'm wedged under there. The closet? Maybe.

I can hear a clash of keys fall on the front steps and the intruder groan as he picks them up. How did Knox get a key? It shouldn't surprise me that he managed. I've seen the lengths he's gone to just to track down men who've tried to screw him out of cash. He would brag to me about how he found them, how he finished them himself, so people would hear of it and know not to fuck with him. He took a lot of pride in winning the game of cat and mouse, and even more pride in slowly, painfully extracting his revenge.

That was just about money. I shot him in the leg, stole his car, took his hidden stash of cash and left a man who thought he owned my body. No, not just my body. My soul.

The front door creaks open and someone stomps inside, bumping up against the counter and thumping into the wall.

Fuck.

It has to be Knox. Jake wouldn't be crashing around his own place. He knows where the fucking counter is in his own kitchen. I leap across the bedroom floor on my tiptoes and try to contain the screams of terror welling up inside me as I stand behind the door. At least here, if he comes in the room, I can try to escape. If I lock myself in a closet, it's too easy for him to grab me. To control me. Like he always has.

Did he kill Jake?

Tears spring to my eyes for the thousandth time today. My hands tremble as I twist my fingers around the hilt of the knife and listen.

"Hey! Holly? Anyone ho-ome?" He calls out as he thumps down the hallway, with the grace of a stampeding bull. His body thuds against the wall and my mind reels. That's not Knox's voice. Not unless he's trying to disguise it. I know I haven't heard him speak in over two months, but I will never forget the voice of evil.

"Hey! Holly!" The doorknob rattles and my mind spins out of control. Did he send someone else to bring me to him?

As the bedroom door squeaks open, I push all thoughts from my mind. It's not time to think. It's time to do.

I raise the knife over my head, prepared to sink it into the throat of whoever Knox has sent to find me. The door flies open and a man trips into the room and falls to the floor and I scream.

"Holly? What the fuck!" He yells, staring up at me with his familiar, deep blue eyes. "What are you doing with that knife?"

Lying on the floor, at my feet, isn't Knox. It isn't anyone sent by him either. Instead, it's the man I love. I lower the knife and tears slide down my face. Jake is home. The man I've been terrified was left for dead. The man who was supposed to come back to me hours and hours ago. The man who promised me he'd keep me safe, he's finally here.

And he's drunk.

CHAPTER 31
Holly

"Jesus, Holly, what are you doing?" Jake sits up and manages to get his wobbly legs back under him. I don't answer him, all of my emotions are spilling down my cheeks as my body is drained of energy. I drop the knife I've been clinging to all day to the floor, and my shoulders slump forward.

"What's going on?" Jake presses me. The heat of his boozy breath erupting over me like lava, rooting me to the spot with a horrified look etched to my face.

"You're drunk," I glance up at him.

"I'm not drunk, I had a few drinks," he frowns at me. "Why the fuck are you hiding in the bedroom, trying to attack me with a knife?" He accuses me.

"I wasn't going to attack you," my eyelids are heavy. It's too much. Today has been too much and I can feel myself shutting down.

"That's not what it looked like to me," Jake points to

the knife on the floor. "What did you think you were gonna do with that, huh?" The edge in his voice grows sharp. "I come back to my own fucking house, a house I let you stay in, and you try to assault me?" He sways like a strong gust of wind is attacking him.

"Jake, I can't do this right now. Not when you're like this. I just… I fucking can't." I wipe the tears from my cheeks and start to turn away.

"Don't walk away from me," Jake circles his broad hand over my wrist and I instinctively raise my arm to cover my face. Like a dog cowering in a corner.

"Don't," I cry out.

Shame washes over me as I watch the mixed emotions on Jake's face. He drops my arm and steps back as hurt wins the battle, making him wince like I really did cut him with the knife. "I'm not him, Holly." His voice is cool. "I wasn't going to hurt you."

"You already did," anger wells up inside me as it hits me that he's been out relapsing for the past six hours while I've been living a nightmare. "You left me here, when Knox is trying to get me, you didn't call, I didn't know where you were, and what were you doing? Getting hammered? Are you fucking kidding me? Did you get high too?" I can't contain my anger. My betrayal.

"High? No, of course not. Why are you freaking out? I just had a few drinks," he lies. I can see from his glassy eyes and flushed face that he's had more than a few. "What the fuck is your problem? You know you're safe here, you don't have to freak out just because I'm a little late coming home. Why do you have a knife? It doesn't make any fucking sense," he rubs his temples.

"Keep me safe? That's a fucking joke, right? Guess

what, Jake," my voice is shrill, and I feel myself teetering on the edge of my sanity, "he found me. He took a fucking picture of us at the grocery store and e-mailed it to me." I point down the hallway.

"What?" Jake blinks blankly.

"Knox knows where I am. He knows I'm with you. You told me you'd keep me safe. What a fucking joke! The first day you go back to work you take off for hours, don't call me, don't answer my calls and get drunk? And I'm supposed to feel safe?" I throw my hands in the air. "How the fuck are you supposed to keep me safe when you can't even look after yourself?" I may not have attacked him with the knife, but I can see my words pierce his heart.

Jake runs his flat palms over his face and then back through his hair. "You're right," he sighs and drops his head. "You're fucking right, I haven't kept my word. And now that son-of-a-bitch knows where you are. Fuck!" He cracks his fist into the doorframe with a sickening thud.

"Why did you go out after work instead of coming home? Why didn't you call me?" My voice is steady despite how weak I feel right now.

"It's," he runs his red hand over the back of his neck and drops his gaze to the floor, "it's complicated," he mumbles.

"It doesn't look that way from where I'm standing. Looks like you wanted to get fucked up." I set my jaw, determined not to feel sorry for whatever lame excuse he's going to toss my way for his piss-poor decision. Literally, the first chance he gets, he fucks off and chooses a night of drinking over me. Over his sobriety? Nothing about that sounds complicated. It just sounds pathetic.

My thoughts trickle through me, burning me like acid as anger wells up inside.

"I did want to get fucked up, I needed to get some distance."

"From me? What the fuck?" I yell.

"Not from you, from the fucking images in my head. Ok? I went to work and they want to send me on deployment again. I can't do it. I can't go back, I still can't stop dreaming about the last time. Every fucking night, it's the same dream!" He shakes his head like a dog flicking off the rain. Like he's trying to fling the thoughts from his brain.

"What are you talking about?" I watch him carefully, feeling myself soften.

Jake looks up at me, tears lining his eyes and my heart breaks as one falls over onto his cheek. "I can't stay in the military anymore, I can't do it. I need help, Holly. Rehab wasn't enough, it didn't make the dreams stop. It wasn't enough." His voice cracks and I close the distance between us, throwing my arms around him.

"What are you talking about? What happened, Jake?"

He slumps over in my arms, "I can't do another deployment. Not after the last one. I don't want to do this anymore." Another tear falls down his face and worry swirls in my gut.

"Jake, please, tell me what's wrong," I beg.

"Holly, my last mission was a success, I got a medal. A fucking medal," he shakes his head. "And a lifetime of nightmares. Cause when we took out one of the top leaders of the Taliban the fucking coward armed his boys. His fucking kids." Jake's voice breaks and he clenches his jaw as tears trail slowly down into his beard. "It was me or him, but I can't stop seeing it. I can't stop hearing it. I know I had no choice, I know that." He shakes his head slowly from side to side and closes his eyes. "I had no choice, but it doesn't matter cause now I'm all fucked up and I can't get it out of my head," he hits his balled-up hand against his forehead.

"Jake," my throat hurts and I hold him. I don't know what to say. I don't know what to ask. I'm not sure I want to know. I had no idea he's been living with this horrible burden all this time. Guilt swirls inside me as I realize that I just assumed all this time that Jake was in because he liked to party. I never bothered to find out about the pain he's lived with all this time. The pain that he carries with him every day.

"I shot him," he whispers, "I killed a little boy over there. A fucking kid. He had a loaded gun, and he was going to shoot me," he doesn't open his eyes as he explains.

"Then you had no choice!" I run my hands over his shoulders.

"It doesn't matter though. I wish he would've killed me instead. Instead of me reliving the hell every night. Seeing it over and over. I can't... I just can't do it anymore. I can't stay in the SEALs. I can't do another deployment. I just want to get my head straight and live a peaceful life. With you. If you'll still have me," he finally opens his eyes and I look up into the pain sweeping behind the intense blue. How have I never noticed it before?

"Of course. We'll get through this, together. Together," I lean into him and he wraps his arms around me.

Somehow, we'll get through it all. As long as we're

together.

CHAPTER 32

Jake

Pulling air deep into my lungs, I walk down the hall to my chief's office. My guts are rolling up inside me like a nest of snakes. Nerves. They're getting to me.

I remember when I was an ambitious eighteen-year-old with more balls than brains and a burning desire in my belly to prove myself. The military was always my plan, but the SEALs, that was my dream. I didn't want to be a run-of-the-mill ground pounder. My father and my big brother had already blazed that path. I didn't want to get lost in their shadows, and a world renowned elite force like the SEALs doesn't sit in anyone's shade.

My hand twitches and I give it a shake before balling it up and knocking on my chief's door. This is it.

The door slides away from me as he opens it. "Armstrong? What is it?" He looks over my shoulder to see if there's some kind of explanation for my interruption of his day.

"Chief," I clear my throat like I did when I was a teenager and I didn't want my voice to betray me by cracking when I talked to a girl. "Do you have a minute?"

He looks me over, his eyebrows scrunching together with concern and then steps back, opening a path to his desk. "Of course, come in," he closes the door behind me and takes a seat. "Sit your ass down, Armstrong and spill it," he nods at the empty seat across from him. "I haven't got all day," his usual gruff tone returns.

I smile and do as I'm told. His salty sailor routine hasn't got me fooled. Don't get me wrong, I'm not stupid enough to go flapping my gums about it, but I know Chief Warrant Officer Andrews well enough to see that he has a good heart under his crusty shell.

"Well, are you gonna sit there smirking at me? Or did you have something you wanted to talk about?"

I puff up my chest, willing the words on the tip of my tongue to spill from my mouth. This is harder than I thought it would be. My mind flashes to last night, lying in bed with Holly.

"Come to the wedding with me. Come to Florida," I urged her.

"What about Knox?"

"He already knows you're here. You're safer with me. Come with me and I'll keep you safe." I continued.

I didn't tell her the other reason I wanted her to. The selfish reason. The one that had nothing to do with Knox, or the wedding, or any of that. That I couldn't stand the idea of being away from her.

I realize now, that the feeling I once had for the SEALs, it's hers now. She has my heart. My mind. My soul. I breathe for her.

She was quiet for so long, I thought she fell asleep. Finally, she answered, "Yes. I'll go. But, I need to do one thing."

"What's that?" I asked.

"I need to see my parents."

I give my head a shake and ground myself into the present moment. Holly's soft, beautiful face evaporates and instead, my chief's deeply etched, angry skin fills my vision.

"Sorry, I, uh, I guess I'm a bit nervous," I confess.

The Chief's face doesn't change; his lips barely move as he tells me to get on with it.

"I wanted to let you know that I've decided not to re-up when my contract expires. I won't be signing the next one, I'm leaving the SEALs." I look down at my hands. I can't handle the mixture of surprise and hint of betrayal spreading across his face.

"You're leaving? Your re-enlistment is coming, when?"

"In two months," I fill in the blank for him.

"In two months," he echoes back, his voice void of emotion. I can feel his hard stare, it's impossible to avoid. "You want to explain to me what the hell this is about?" Andrews tilts his head.

I squirm in my seat a bit, "It's a lot of things." I meet his penetrating gaze, forcing myself to lay all the cards on the table. "I'm having problems sleeping. I have nightmares, all the time. I want to get help for that," I start.

"Well, that's nothing new around here. We can get you that help," he cuts in.

"It's more than that. I met someone. I love her, and I realize that my heart's not in this anymore. I want to get my head straight and be the best man I can for her. And that includes actually being there for her. I know, even if I get these dreams under control, I'll still be gone all the time. At a moment's notice, I'll be walking out of her life. Never knowing when I'm going to walk back in it. I can't do it." I confess.

A twinkle shines in Chief Warrant Officer Andrews' eyes and he leans back in his chair, "A girl, huh? You're going to throw away your career, everything you built up for yourself, for a woman?" He squints his eyes at me.

"Yes. I am, Chief."

I watch as he twists back and forth in his chair, chewing on what I just told him. "Listen, Armstrong, I get it. Ok? We've all been there. This hasn't been your year, you know. You had your Captain's Mast, you went off to rehab, and now you've got a head full of treatment and a heart full of lust."

He shuffles a bunch of folders on his desk, searching for something. Plucking a sheet of paper from one, leaning forward, he thrusts it over to me. "Look, your leave pass is approved to go to your brother's wedding, ok? How about you go see your family, and think about this some more. Make damned sure that this isn't just some leftover crisis from the shit year you've had, ok?"

I look from the stamped leave pass to his wrinkled face and nod. "I will. I'll make sure, but I know my mind won't change." I stare into his brown eyes.

"You sound pretty confident, but just make sure. You know, once you're out, you won't be getting back in with us."

"I know."

Chief Andrews relaxes back into his seat and smiles, "All right. You sound pretty sure of yourself, so I will say one thing. Take it from someone who's sitting on the other side of their career from where you are, there's only room for one."

"Chief?" I wait for him to explain.

"You can be married to a woman who steals your heart, or the SEALs. Both never work together. Take it from me, I've found three different women who were crazy enough to walk down the aisle with me, and not one of them stuck."

I look down at the paper in my hands, "Ok. Thanks, Chief." I stand up to leave.

"Oh, and Armstrong?"

"Yes," I turn back to face him.

"Take it from someone who thought he found 'the one' three times; make damned sure you're doing the right thing. I'd hate to see you throw it all away just to end up with a lifetime of regrets," he answers.

"Yes, Chief."

"Now, get outta here," he flips his hand at me. "And close the door behind you, I don't need any more fucking interruptions!" His gruff tone returns with a vengeance.

I smile and walk out of his office, letting the door click behind me. I've never felt more certain of anything before. Holly is the one, there's no second-guessing that.

Yet, as I make my way back down the hall, I can't help the small, nagging voice that intrudes my thoughts and twists in my gut.

What if… what if I'm wrong?

Chapter 33

Jake

"That's my exit," Holly points at the green freeway sign announcing Everglades City in another fifteen miles.

"Gotcha," I nod, giving her a smile. She doesn't return it though, instead she goes back to staring out her window.

I can see this trip is taking an emotional toll on her and we haven't even gotten there.

"Hey, don't worry, ok? I'm not going to be far away. If you call me, I'll be there for you. I'm only a couple of hours down the road." I try to reassure her about the distance that we agreed to allow between us tonight.

Holly was adamant about going to her parents' house before continuing on to Miami for the wedding stuff. I can understand where she's coming from, even if it does make me nervous to leave her in Everglades City while I take my brother out for his bachelor party in Miami. Her family has been torn apart for over five years, more if you count the time they were all grieving her sister's death before Holly even took off. They need some time together. I get that, but it still makes me uneasy.

"I know, I'm just full of butterflies, you know? I'm nervous. It just feels like everything is a bit of a mess right now." She smiles at me weakly.

"Listen, I've got you. If you need a break from your parents, or you hear from Knox, it doesn't matter, I'll be there. I promise," I lift her hand to my lips, softly kissing the back.

Her smile grows stronger, but it's still forced. "Besides," I continue, "I don't want to brag or anything," I look at her from the corner of my eye with a half-cocked smile on my lips.

"You? I couldn't imagine," she teases me.

"Exactly, I'm obviously too humble for that. Probably the humblest person you know, to be honest." I joke.

"Oh, definitely," her eyes twinkle.

"Anyway, not only are you with probably one of the toughest, strongest and handsomest Navy SEALs of all time," I smile.

"So humble," she laughs.

"But, you're also in the presence of the baddest gangster the East side has."

"Oh, is that a fact," she shakes her head. "How's that?"

"Well, not to toot my own horn, of course." I pick up my iPod and search through my old tried and true tracks until I find the song I'm looking for.

"You? Never," she smirks and it makes me happy to see the worry finally disappear from her eyes, even if it's only temporary.

"Right, but I can spit some mad rhymes, yo." I hit the play button and my speakers fill with the familiar opening to my jam.

"Under Pressure? By Queen?" She looks at me confused.

"Nope!" I pretend to pick up an old-school mic, and belt out the opening line with way too much enthusiasm.

Holly can't contain her laughter as the track fills the car with whispers of "Ice, Ice Baby."

I sing Vanilla Ice's masterpiece as I pull off onto the exit for Holly's hometown. Holly is pretending she isn't impressed, but I can tell her admiration is barely contained beneath the surface. I look over at her and she watches me, amused. Holly leans forward and turns the music down to a hush, but I keep singing along.

"Why the hell do you know all the words to Ice, Ice Baby?" She laughs.

"I told ya, I'm a straight up gangster!" I tease her.

"No, seriously," she smiles and I'm happy to see the pain and fear are finally free from her gorgeous blue eyes.

"Well, besides the fact that it's probably one of the greatest songs of all time, you mean?" I smirk.

"Yeah, besides that," she tilts her head and her long hair cascades down over her shoulders.

"I had an overly arty teacher that incorporated it into our school Christmas play one year. As the head elf of the Ice Brigade, I needed to learn all the words," I confess.

"Wow, you are the original gangster," she laughs.

"Told you," I squeeze her hand. I've hated seeing Holly so consumed by her fears and sadness. I've been trying to lighten the mood whenever I can. Besides, it helps me keep my mind off my own demons when I help her forget hers.

The worst times are when she just disappears into her shell though. Where I can't reach her. I hate how I can see the agony play out on her face like a movie screen, knowing it was pain he caused her. Most of the time, she'll talk about it. About how he beat her, controlled her, took away her spirit. The rage boils up inside me when I think about what he's done to her. As difficult as it is to listen to what she's been through, it's harder still when she won't talk about it. When she just cries or silently stares, refusing to say a word. Those are the times I know death is far too good for Knox. However, I'll have no problem delivering it, if I get the chance.

Holly's smile fades as she looks at what must be a trip down memory lane for her. "My parents' house is just down this street," she points to the sign on the corner and I flip on the signal.

"Are you sure you want to spend the night here? I can still bring you to Miami with me." I offer, but she shakes her head stubbornly.

"No, this is something I need to do," she answers firmly.

"Ok." I drive slowly down the street of large houses with perfectly manicured lawns. "Which one is it?" I look over at her. She's staring out the window again, but this time I know it's not about Knox. No one should ever live with as much pain as she has in her life. I wish I could carry it all for her, every scar, and every memory. I hate knowing even half of what she's been through.

"It's down further," she mumbles, her full lips flat line and her rosy cheeks pale. "Jake?"

"Yeah?"

"Promise me you'll stay sober. I know it's a bachelor party and there's going to be a lot of temptation. Just, please, promise me?" She searches my face and my gut twists up in a knot. I can't stand myself right now. The fact that she feels like she has to ask me this makes self-loathing and shame rush through my veins. I hate that I gave her any reason to doubt me. I never wanted to add another layer to her worries.

"I promise." I whisper. "You have my word," I answer simply, looking her in the eyes.

"Thank you," she lets out the breath I didn't realize she was holding. "Ok, this one, with the red car," she points to a driveway ahead, "that's my parents' house."

I pull in and recognize her mother immediately sitting on the hammock, reading. She looks much older looking, but is still gorgeous. She jumps up with a surprise upon noticing our arrival.

"There's Mom," Holly explains.

We watch as her mother starts to walk over to the car and then stops, blatantly staring at us before turning on her heel and speed walking into the house.

"Looks like this is going to go well," she says dryly.

"Are you sure you want to stay here tonight?" I ask again, throwing the car in park. "You're allowed to change your mind, you know." I press her.

"It'll be fine," she forces a smile. The front door of the house flings back open and Holly's father bounds outside, waving at us happily.

Holly unbuckles her seatbelt and slides out of the car, letting her father consume her in his bear hug. I walk over to their side of the car and hold out my hand, he takes a second to see it, but gives me a firm shake.

"It's good to see you again, Sir." I smile.

"You too. And I'm so happy to see you, Holly," he throws his arm over her shoulder, smiling.

"I'll grab your bag," I offer, but her father holds up his hand. "No, I'll let you two say your goodbyes, let me grab it instead." He doesn't wait for an answer, walking over to the back door of my car, he plucks her bag from the seat and takes it into the house.

"Thanks, Dad!" Holly calls out and her father waves it off.

"Ok, well, if you need anything, I'm only a phone call away." I hold her chin between my finger and thumb, tilting her head up to me and kiss her tenderly.

Holly melts into my arms as our tongues briefly collide. I pull back, resting my forehead against hers and she sighs. "It's going to be fine," she promises.

"I know, I just hate to leave you," I admit.

"Knox doesn't know where I'm from," she squeezes my hand reassuring me for the tenth time.

I watched carefully while I was driving, keeping an eye out for any cars on our tail, but nothing. Still, I can't shake the feeling that she'd be better off with me.

"I love you, Jake," she whispers.

"I love you, too." I run my hand through her hair and smile. "So much."

I give her another quick kiss and force myself to get back into the car. As I back out of the driveway, I can't help but feel like I'm making a mistake. Like I should grab her and take her with me, rather than leave her with a hostile mother and a ton of bad blood. Holly raises her hand to wave and I wave back, driving away, watching her shrink in the rearview mirror as I go.

"She'll be ok, you can't protect her from everything," I tell myself, but the words fall flat when my heart, my gut and every fiber of my being is telling me differently. "It's only one night. Just one night," I repeat. As I drive away, I hope that this one night apart isn't the one that destroys us.

CHAPTER 34

Holly

"Have you made any friends yet? Are the neighbors nice?" Dad mops up the last of the sauce on his plate with a homemade bun as he continues to carry the conversation.

"No, I haven't really made any friends yet, but everyone seems nice enough," I answer.

"Are you going to get a job, or just keep sponging off Jake?" My mother's tone is an Arctic blast despite the early summer Florida heat.

"Beverly," my father hisses.

"It's all right, Dad." I wave away his instinct to jump in. "I haven't been looking for a job yet, I'm actually thinking of finishing off my schooling. I think I'd like to go to college too," I force a smile across my face and my mother doesn't bat an eye. Not a single muscle twitches in her face as she stares me down across the table.

"College! That's wonderful, honey!" My father exclaims, clapping his hands together loudly. "What for?"

"I think I'd like to look into working with animals. I don't think I could be a vet, but maybe a veterinary assistant. I don't know, I'm still figuring it all out, to be honest." I look down at my empty plate. I helped myself to a second serving of Mom's home cooking.

It's funny, she's been nothing but an ice queen to me since I walked in the door. I tried to give her a hug earlier and I'm pretty sure I have frostbite on my arms now. Yet, the Ice Queen still went out of her way to make my favorite meal. Veggie lasagna with smoked Gouda cheese on top. Between my mother's sub-zero welcome and the meal, I couldn't help but remember a simpler time in our family. Back when my sister and I used to play outside on January afternoons and come home to this very meal.

Simpler times indeed.

Mom stands up from the table and begins clearing the empty plates from my father and me. "Here, let me help you with that," I offer, sliding my chair back and hopping to my feet.

"I don't need any help, I'm used to clearing the table myself." She shuts me down and grabs her stack of dishes like they're a precious jewel I'm trying to pluck from her hands.

I ignore her and pick up the glasses and cutlery, following her into the kitchen close on her heels. Mom leans over the kitchen sink as the hot water pours into it from the tap and she sighs deeply. I slide the glasses and silverware onto the counter next to her and her head snaps up like an angry jack-in-the-box.

"What are you doing?"

"I'm helping you clear the table, why? What's the big

deal?"

"The big deal is that I told you to leave it alone!" She yells, her face flushing red.

"Whatever, why did you even ask me to come visit you guys. You obviously don't want me here. It was a mistake to come back," the forks and knives clink loudly as I drop them down next to her.

"Yeah, maybe it was a mistake," her words knock my head back with the invisible punch they carry.

"Beverly! What are you doing?" My father stands in the doorway, his voice booming through the room.

"I'm sorry, but I'm not going to just act like everything is fixed because she's decided to grace us with her presence for a night. It still doesn't make up for any of it." She looks from my father to me, leveling me with her glare, "It still doesn't fix what you did!" She points her finger at me like she's trying to stab me in the heart. That would probably hurt less than this.

"I never should have come here," I can't stand to look at her face, twisted up with rage and disgust. I turn around and cross the kitchen floor, pushing past my dad in the doorway.

Hot tears splash over my burning cheeks as I blindly make my way through the house. I don't bother listening to the argument they're having, to the actual words attached to the growing noise coming from them. Instead, I grab my coat, slip on my shoes and walk out the front door.

I don't know where I'm going to go. I don't care. I just need to get out of there. She hates me. My own mother hates me.

And I can't even blame her.

CHAPTER 35

Holly

I'm not sure how long I've been walking the empty streets of my small town. Nothing here seems to have changed one bit. It's not even nine o'clock and this place makes a funeral parlor look like a hip hot spot.

Nothing has changed, I remind myself. My family is still as fucked up as before I ever left for Miami. It's like we've all taken our pain and locked it into a time capsule, preserving every detail as fresh as the day we buried it.

I look up and come to a full stop as I realize where my feet have taken me. I've been in such a fog of memories and emotions that I haven't even been paying attention to where I was going. My heart must have guided the way. Fresh tears fill my eyes as I look at the train bridge where my sister died.

I've never come back here. I just couldn't do it; the memories were already too much to live with. I'm not sure if it's courage or stupidity that propels me forward now, but either way, I can't seem to stop my feet from closing the distance between me and the bridge.

For the first time since that night, I walk to the edge of the bank and look down to the water below that took Heather's life. I struggle to breathe as the details from that night crash over me like a tidal wave.

"Did you come here to freak everyone out, or what?" I demanded. Heather was sitting off to the side, watching us like Jane Goodall researching a bunch of chimps instead of being a normal teenager at a party.

"I'm not freaking anyone out," she stuck out her chin, but her eyes darted around at the crowd of underage drinkers behind me, searching for proof of my words.

"Yes, you are," I took a huge gulp of the ridiculously strong rum and coke in my red Solo cup, and thrust another one, that was just as terribly mixed, under her nose. "You're at a party, have some fun for once. Don't just sit here like a plant. There are cute guys here tonight, let's have some fun!" I pushed her.

"It's just not my thing," she grasped the cup in her hand and wrinkled her nose at the smell.

"Yeah, and how's 'your thing' working out for you? God, you've got no friends, no boyfriend, and you're bringing everyone down here. Why don't you try a different thing for once? I know, you can do 'my thing' for tonight and go have some fun for once in your life," I egged her on.

"Oh, what's that? Get drunk and make out with every guy here? No thanks," she snarked.

"Yeah! Exactly! Have some fun! Be young! Stop acting like you're ninety-two. God, we're sixteen and our parents are out of town for the weekend. Get crazy! Let your hair down for once." I finished the nasty drink in my cup.

"I wouldn't know what to do anyway," Heather shrugged, giving up. But, I wasn't taking no for an answer.

Why didn't I just leave her alone?

"Ok, step one: drink up. Step two: get off your ass and have some fun. There you go, there's your insider tips on how to be a normal teenager for once. Come on, we're going to go climb on the guardrails under the bridge and smoke a joint, just come with us." I held out my hand to help her off the ground.

"Nah, I'll just wait for you here," she looked down at the ground.

"No! No way! It's time to stop acting like such an old granny. Listen, I dare you, I double-dog, twin dare you to get up and come with us. Come on, what's the worst that could happen? You could have some fun? You know you gotta now, it's a dare. You can't turn down a double-dog, twin dare. There's like a law or something," I joked.

The pressure was too much. Heather shrugged, gulped back her entire drink, and she never drank, then hopped to her feet. I should've known that the liquor would hit her hard. I should've let her sit and watch the party in peace. Instead, I bullied her into doing what I wanted.

I'm not sure how much more booze she drank, but I knew she was tipsy when I watched her kiss Josh Rexton on the lips. Heather was a shy girl, so quiet and so camouflaged into the background that a lot of people didn't even realize I had a twin. Kissing a high school senior wasn't her style. Nothing about that night was her style.

I shouldn't have let her climb out there first. She was feeling the booze and acting crazy. I told her to wait, but she jumped up on the metal guardrail and started shuffling her feet as she gripped hand-over-hand out toward the middle of the bridge. It was hard to see much more than her silhouette, but I could still hear her.

"There ya go!" She yelled back at me. "Double-dog twin dare accomplished," she leaned back and everyone started yelling on the shore.

"Hey, be careful!" I cried in alarm.

I could only see her dark outline as she lost her grip. Her screams penetrated the air and then nothing after the splash.

"Heather!" I shrieked, running down to the bank. "Heather, oh shit! Someone has to save her. I'm going in. Heather!" I screamed so loud my throat burned.

I don't remember who held me back. I just remember the strong arms circling my waist. "You'll get swept away by the current, you can't jump in."

I remember I fought with all of my strength to be freed.

They didn't find her body until the next day.

Tears stream down my face, soaking my shirt. "I'm sorry, Heather," I whisper to the water. "I'm so sorry."

"I thought I would find you here."

My heart leaps in my chest as I whirl around on my heel. "Mom?"

"Yeah, I figured you might come down here. I come here when I get upset too." She looks past me at the water that stole her child's life and guilt consumes me.

Neither of us move. We're statues under the starry sky. The only noise in the air is the water flowing below.

Mom wipes the back of her hand over her face and I realize she's been crying too. "Listen, Holly, about tonight," she begins but I can't bring myself to hear her say it. I hold up my hands, willing her to stop before she can tell me what I already know.

"I know, you hate me," I interrupt.

"What?"

"It's obvious. I don't blame you. I know you never forgave me for Heather's death. I dared her to cross the bridge that night. It's my fault she died. I understand why you can't forgive that." The words tumble from my mouth, spilling like blood from a cut artery.

"You think I hate you? That I blame you?" She shakes her head slowly like she's translating the words from a different language.

"Please, let's not do this. Like you said, it was a mistake for me to come here. Let's just go back to the house and I'll be out of your hair first thing in the morning," I promise her.

"Woah, stop right there, young lady," her sharp tone makes my muscles freeze as my feet root to the spot. "You think that all this time I've been angry with you about some stupid dare you and your sister made? That I thought you were to blame for a dumb accident?"

I blink like I'm trying to communicate in Morse code. Of course that's what I thought. It's what I still think.

"You listen to me," Mom grabs my shoulders and shakes me, "I never hated you. I never blamed you for anything to do with Heather's death. Never," she emphasizes the word. "You broke my heart, Holly." She lets go of my arms and looks down at the ground, "You shattered it. Not because of your sister, because of you. I was already grieving for her when you took off. You didn't call. I didn't know where you were. For five years, I had no idea if you were even alive. Five years," her voice cracks and fat tears fall to her cheeks. "Do you have any idea what that felt like?"

I don't. I stare down at my feet, trying for the first time to put myself in my mother's place. I was always so wrapped up in my own guilt and self-loathing that it never occurred to me that she still loved me. "No." I finally whisper.

"I felt like I didn't just lose one daughter that night, but both of my little girls. I felt like you died right along with her. You disappeared for five years, then you showed up on our doorstep like nothing happened. I barely had time to adjust to the idea that you were still alive and you were off to Canada for rehab. Then, we go all the way up there to find out that you were taking off again. That you weren't coming back into my life. It didn't even seem like it was something you wanted. Just 'poof' gone again."

My heart hurts as I realize the pain I've caused my mother. I was so wrapped up in my own suffering to see what I had put her through. All this time, I was convinced that she hated me… so much wasted time that I can never get back.

I cover my face with my hands and struggle to breathe as I sob. My shoulders shake and my nose runs all over the place as the tears burst out from the dam I've built up inside. "I'm so sorry, Mom. I'm sorry." I repeat over and over.

My mother steps toward me and wraps her arms around me as I bawl against her shoulder like I did when I was a little girl with scraped knees and a banged up Barbie bike. "Shhh, it's ok, baby. It's ok," her voice chokes up as she rocks me back and forth. "I love you so much, Holly. I love you, hun." She soothes me.

"I love you too, Mom."

CHAPTER 36

Jake

I glance around the nearly empty pub, then back to my brother's face. "This isn't much of a bachelor party, Cameron. You sure you don't want us to take you out to Miami Beach or something?" This place is dead. Of course, it doesn't help that it's only nine at night. Before rehab, nine was when I'd go grab a shower to start getting ready to go out. Most of the time, I didn't even hit the clubs until after eleven, usually finding my way home, with at least one random girl on my arm as the sun came up.

"Nah, the guys on the team took me out for a wild night last week. Bottle service, models hanging at our table, the whole nine. I just wasn't feeling it, you know? It's just not who I am anymore, I guess I've settled down in my old age," Cameron smiles and takes a long sip of his beer.

I get that. Thinking back to how I used to live feels like watching a movie of someone else's life now. A train wreck of a movie at that. Partying all the time used to be my escape. My attempt to add a little color to the gray swamp I was sinking into. The thing is, you can dress up your ugly truth however you want, but it doesn't change it. You can put a turd on the most delicious, home-baked bread and throw a million pictures of it up on Instagram with the best filters, but it's still a shit sandwich.

Holly and rehab helped me see that I needed to change what was going on inside to really enjoy anything life had to offer. I know I've still got work to do, but now that I've had a taste of what a fulfilling life can feel like, I won't be going back to turds on rye anytime soon.

"Doesn't mean you're old, and you sure as shit ain't settled. Just means you're in love," Mack nods at Cameron. The two of them have been best friends since they served together in Afghanistan. My brother was a ground pounder over there and Mack was his officer. Years before that, they both graduated high school the same year, and now that they're both retired from the service, their friendship has gone full circle.

"Couldn't agree with you more, brother," Cameron smiles at his old friend. "I don't want to go out to some club and get my dick grinded by a random chick. Not when I have perfection waiting for me at the altar tomorrow," he takes another drink. "Besides, why would I want to go out on the town like some kind of frat boy when I've got my real brothers here? This is better than some wild night I'd probably regret."

I take a gulp of my Pepsi. Not rum and Pepsi. Not rye and Pepsi. Just regular soda and ice. It still feels weird to be at a bar without drinking. I'll take 'weird' over the twisting knife of guilt slicing through my guts any day. I promised Holly I would stay sober, but more importantly, I promised myself.

"I can't believe you're getting married tomorrow," I shake my head. "It's even crazier that you're going to be a dad soon," I smile. "When is Chelsea due again?"

"Beginning of August. If it all works out right, we'll be married before summer camp starts for me and the baby should be here before the season starts in the fall."

"Sounds like it was all meant to be. You're having an amazing year, Cameron. I'm proud of you. I'm sorry I couldn't be there for your draft," I look down at the sturdy wooden table we're all leaning on.

"Don't be. I'm proud of you too, man. You got your shit sorted out, dealt with it head on. Besides, you're still my best man, right? That's the main thing."

"True," I sit up straighter, feeling less like a loser with my unmixed drink.

"Yeah, just throwing it out there, but I got robbed, by the way," Mack smirks at me.

"What?"

"I mean, I made him my best man at my wedding," he jerks his thumb at my big brother, "but then when it's his turn to get married he chooses you." He jokes.

"Well, we are related and all that," I shrug.

"Nepotism," Mack laughs. "It's supposed to be the best man for the job, not the best sibling," he takes a drink of his beer.

"He did," I shoot back, "can't help it if I'm so good I win both titles."

Mack laughs good naturedly and claps his hand on my shoulder, "You're right, he did. I'm just fucking around."

"Well, it means a lot to me that you're both going to be there. The world, actually." Cameron leans in and looks at us earnestly.

"Wouldn't have it any other way, man." I answer. Mack nods in agreement.

Cameron clears his throat loudly and slides his chair back. "Ok, enough of that," he let's out a dry laugh. "I'll go get us another round," he throws his broad shoulders back and strolls over to the bar.

Mack and I sit in silence for a moment, then he tilts his head and looks at me, "So how are things now that you're back? You've been pretty quiet about returning to your unit."

I take a sharp breath, not prepared to let go of the secret that I've been holding onto. That I'm leaving the SEALs. It's not that I'm ashamed of my decision or anything, it's just that this is my brother's night and I didn't want to make it all about me.

"Uh, I'm not sure." I do a terrible job at avoiding the question.

"You're not sure?" He presses me.

"Well, I guess I am sure. I just, well I haven't told my family yet, but I'm not re-enlisting. My contract runs out in a couple of months and that's it for me," I admit. My body feels lighter after letting go of the burden of truth.

"Why's that?" Mack is no idiot, he knows he's making me uncomfortable. So, why is he pushing this so hard?

"It's just not for me, things have changed." I fling a flimsy excuse back at him.

"What changed?"

My eyes snap up at him, silently demanding that he let

this go, but he doesn't back down.

"I've just got other things I want to do now. Besides, now that Holly and I are together, I don't want to be deploying all the time, you know?" I give him half the truth. "Why, what's with all the questions?" I flip the tables, seeing how he likes being put on the spot.

"All right! Got two beers and a soda." Cameron interrupts, plopping the drinks down on the table.

"Thanks, man," I look up at my brother, happy for the distraction to Mr. Twenty-questions over there.

"Yeah, no problem. I'm just gonna take a piss, I'll be back," he peels off again leaving me in an awkward silence with Mack.

"Look man, it's none of my business or anything," Mack begins.

"Yep." My tone is sharp.

"Right, but I can't help but notice you've got that stare, Jake." He continues.

"What stare?" I look up at him, letting some of my irritation slide away into curiosity.

"That million-mile stare, man. The one you get when you've seen shit you can't unsee. Now, I don't know if that's the case. I don't know if that's part of the reason you're getting out," he raises his hands like I'm pointing a gun at him. "I'm just saying it looks like you've got it. I would know. I've been there," he confesses.

I remember his struggle well. He came back from the war a national hero, and it didn't take long for the media coverage on him to change when he had a huge PTSD flashback and tried to drag someone out of their car. The backlash was swift, until Cooper Sanders, the famous news anchor interviewed him and Mack admitted he needed help.

"I know you do," I nod. "I, uh, well…" My gaze blurs and I rub my hands over my face, anxious to make this, to make all of this, this conversation, this pain, these memories that haunt me, this endless feeling of guilt, all of it, go away. "Yeah, I'm dealing with that shit too," I finally let the truth spill free.

Mack just nods, pulls his wallet out and plucks a card from within. "Here," he hands it over to me, "A few years ago, I was in your shoes. I wish someone would've let me know about Wounded Warriors before it all broke me, man. I went to them for help, and now I work for them. My life's never been better. Think about it, ok?"

I turn the card over in my hands. It feels like I just won a fucking golden ticket. Maybe this is my way out. My chance to finally break through the surface of the sea of horrors I'm drowning in and pull that first breath of fresh air into my burning lungs.

"Thanks, Mack," I run my thumb over the card. Maybe the ticket to my freedom.

"No problem. Take it from me, don't wait until you make the wrong kind of headlines before you do something about it. You and your girl deserve better than that." He looks me straight in the eyes.

"You're right, man." I put the card in my own wallet, and feel something that I can't remember feeling in years.

Hope.

"Hey! Why so serious? This is a celebration, not a funeral!" Cameron squeaks his chair across the hardwood and plunks back down on it.

"Hey man, if it's alright with you, how about we make this our last drink?" Mack looks over at Cameron. "Maybe I am getting old after all, but I'd like to have an early night so I don't look like a bag of shit at your wedding tomorrow."

"Well, you do want to look pretty for all the pictures, right?" Cameron teases him.

"Exactly. Gotta get that beauty sleep," he laughs.

"How about you? You wanna hit the road?" My brother looks across the table at me.

"Huh?" I pull myself from my distracted thoughts about what Mack told me. About new beginnings. About hope.

"Yeah, let's call it." I agree. "Chelsea will have our necks if you ruin her wedding pictures looking like a tired old man," I chuck shit at my brother.

"True," Cameron takes a long swig of his beer. "Very true. Ok, let's roll boys," he laughs. "Nah, I'm just kidding, you can finish your drinks first," Mack and I smile.

As Cameron and Mack finish up their beer, I have a hard time pretending to listen to their conversation. I can't help but let my thoughts drift to an unfamiliar place. To the future. My future. Instead of all of the dread and uncertainty those thoughts are usually weighed down by, for once, I let myself dream of the possibilities.

For once, I have hope.

CHAPTER 37

Jake

"You wanna explain to me how you got kicked out of your own house the night before your wedding?" Mack busts Cameron's chops as I pull the car up to the curb at the front of the hotel.

"I didn't get kicked out. She just didn't want us seeing each other until tomorrow. I guess it's bad luck or some crazy superstition."

"Poor guy," I mock him. "She's got you slumming it here at the Ritz with us while she has your new place to herself."

"Yeah, she's got her Mom with her," Cameron shrugs. "All I know is, you don't argue with a pregnant lady and you don't argue with your fiancée right before the wedding. If your fiancée happens to be a pregnant woman, you suck it up and make her happy. If it's important to her, it's important to me," he gets out of the car. Mack frees himself from the backseat and slams the car door shut as I make my way from the driver's seat. I toss the keys to the valet waiting behind a little podium by the front door, "Hey, Cameron! Tell the guy your room number," I jerk my head in the direction of the hotel staff.

"Right, uh," Cameron pulls out his hotel card and reads off the information, "it's for room eleven-eighty-three." The valet nods and scurries over to the car as the three of us enter the massive glass doors to the lobby.

"Cameron? Jake? Uh, do you guys have a minute?"

"Dad?" We both answer, looking at each other with unasked questions in our eyes.

Why is he waiting for us in the hotel lobby, pouncing out of the shadows the minute we get back? What's going on?

"I should get back to my room," Mack excuses himself from our unexpected family reunion. "Lauren's probably at the end of her rope with the kids," he explains.

"Ok man, I've got wake up calls set for all of the rooms. I'll see you in the morning," my brother calls out to him as Mack crosses the lobby and strolls past the elevators, opting to take the stairs instead.

My attention turns back to my father. It would seem he's finally come out of hiding. I didn't expect to see him until the ceremony tomorrow. Mom came out to dinner with us earlier tonight along with Mack and his family, but she made a lame excuse about why our father couldn't join us.

"So, your headache is all gone then?" I give him a sharp look.

"What?"

"That's what I thought," I mutter.

"Never mind that," Cameron flickers his eyes from my

face to Dad's. "What's going on? Is everything ok?" His voice is full of concern.

"Yes, everything is good. Don't worry. I, uh, well," Dad rubs his hand over the back of his neck and looks down at his feet. "I was hoping I could talk to you boys, if that's ok. I mean, if you're not too busy." He mumbles.

Cameron and I exchange another look. What the hell is this about? I decide to let the chip fall from my shoulder and agree to find out.

"Sure," I answer.

"Yeah Dad, do you guys want to come up to my room and talk?"

"Yeah," Dad answers, "I'd like that."

We make our way to the elevator in silence. The ding of the metal doors sliding open for us is absurdly loud in the noiseless vacuum we've created. Cameron pushes the buttons and we wordlessly travel up to the eleventh floor.

Ding!

Dad and I follow Cameron's lead, down the hall to his room. I can't stop wondering what this is about. Is there some bad news he needs to give to us? Is he dying? I shake the thoughts from my head and settle down on the couch in the living area of my brother's hotel room.

"What's up, Dad?" Cameron prompts our father to break his tense silence and spill it. However, Dad just looks out the window at the twinkling lights of the city below.

"You've got a beautiful view here," he marvels.

"Did you really want to admire the sights, or was there something you wanted to talk about?" I don't mean to snap at him. However, the residue of the last talk I had with my father is still clinging to my heart. Like plaque.

Dad clears his throat loudly and turns around. His eyes are watery and his cheeks are flushed. I instantly feel remorse for giving the old man attitude. Obviously, something is going on with him. I should zip my lips and let him talk at his own pace.

"You're right, just nervous I guess," he slides his hands down over his pants and walks slowly to the couch, sitting down beside me. Cameron plops himself down in the chair opposite us, never taking his eyes off our father.

"Why are you nervous?" I can see my brother's wheels spinning as he ponders the same questions I was just sifting through a minute ago. "Dad, are you ok?" His voice is soft, like he's afraid to ask the question.

"Yes, I am. Well, I will be. I just needed to talk to my boys. It's just," he takes a deep, unsteady breath and looks from Cameron to me, "I wanted to say I'm sorry to you two." His words are shaky and don't make sense to my ears. My father never apologizes. At least, not for as long as I can remember.

"Sorry?" I repeat the word like it's foreign.

"What for, Pops?" Cameron tilts his head.

"Boys, I've had a lot of time to think over the past couple of months. Cameron, you've got your first child, my first grandchild on the way and I guess it's been getting me thinking. I'm an old man now, I've had a long life to reflect on."

"Oh, come on, you're not that old, Dad," Cameron rolls his eyes.

"Maybe not, but you two are grown men now and it's easy to look back and think about all the mistakes I've made raising you both. Cameron, I wasn't very supportive of you going after your football dream, and look at you," Dad raises his hand like he's trying to lift my brother in the palm of his hand, "you made it in the NFL. I told you before how proud I am of you, but I can't say it enough. I'm glad you didn't listen to me," Dad looks up at my brother with shining eyes. I stare at Cameron too, and raise a questioning eyebrow. He never told me that he and my father had a heart-to-heart while I was in rehab. I guess I missed a lot while I was away.

The memory of my father yelling at me on Family Day while I was in rehab comes back to me with a stinging slap. I set my jaw and lower my eyes to the floor as I watch him storm out of the room, out of my recovery and out of my life all over again in my mind.

"Jake," Dad interrupts the memory, "I didn't treat you right when you went to Canada to get help, son. I was just so shocked by your addiction and you getting in trouble that I didn't even focus on the part that mattered the most. That you got the help you needed. I'm proud of you for doing what you needed to get back on track so you can go back to being the best Navy SEAL you can be," his chin lifts with pride as he says that last part. Something inside me wants to take that away from him. To leave him feeling as crushed as he left me when he stomped out of Edgewood that day.

"I'm not staying with the SEALs, Dad," I answer calmly.

"What?" He twists fully around on the couch so he's facing me straight on, his face is contorted like he just stepped on a nail.

"I'm not re-upping. My contract runs out in a couple of months and I'm moving on with my life. It's what's best for me, for my sobriety, for my peace of mind, and for Holly." I tap on a finger for each thing on my list. Dad opens and closes his mouth like a goldfish, but for once he doesn't have anything to say. I've got to admit, it feels good to watch him grapple with my words. To take away something that meant so much to him... too much to him. Just like he was so quick to take away his love as soon as I hit a speed bump on my life's path.

"You never told me that," Cameron darts his eyes over to me.

"This is your time. I didn't want to make it all about me," I confess with a shrug.

Dad sits up straighter, forcing his shoulders back. Here it comes. Let's hear how I'm a fuck up. A failure. How he's not proud of me, or worse.

"Good," he whispers, nodding his head. "That's good, Jake," he repeats louder.

"What?" I feel my moment of victory deflate from my puffed-out chest as my father sticks a pin in it.

"You know what's best for you and your life," Dad looks into my eyes, "I trust you know what you're doing." His voice grows more confident and more convincing. "Besides, I was wrong to push you both into the military anyway, and I know that's why you both joined. I'm not even sure why I did that, if I really think about it," Dad runs his hand over his thinning hair and stares out the hotel window for answers.

"You didn't force us to join. We wanted to," I answer, but when I look over at my brother's face, I can see that I might be wrong.

"It wasn't my first choice," Cameron admits with a shrug.

"I know," Dad looks over at him. "And I was a pretty shitty father when you left too." He answers.

I remember how my father stopped talking to Cameron when he left the military to go back to university. Not like he completely froze him out as much as he started pretending he couldn't really hear him. He stopped making conversation with him. He stopped showing an interest in his life. It was like, when Cameron moved on with his life, Dad held a funeral in his heart for the son he still wished Cameron would be. He never seemed to get over the grief, the betrayal, the anger. Whatever those phases of grief are, Dad never really seemed to get through them. It left a rift in their relationship for years.

"And you," Dad looks back at me, shaking me from my thoughts, "I know I pushed you to go Special Forces. I don't know why, I'm not sure what I was thinking. I don't know if you would've gone for the SEALs if I wouldn't have been so stubborn about it," he looks at me.

"I'm not sure," I look down at my hands. I've never thought about it before.

"Boys, the thing is, you know we come from a long line of military. My grandfather made it to Master Sergeant back in his day. He only had a grade eight education too, so that was pretty good back then. Then he pushed my father to join, and your Granddad took his commission. He was so proud of that." Dad shakes his head and his eyes water. "I never told either of you this before," his voice grows thick, "but I never wanted to join the military. I mean, I did, I reached General and I'm proud of my time, but I never wanted that for my career," he looks over at my brother and me.

It's hard to imagine my father in any other job, or having any other passions. He was always the kind of military dad that would give us 'room inspections' and dress us down like little soldiers when we got in shit. He was never one of those guys who hung it up at work at the end of the day and left his at the door when he got home. He was military through and through.

"What did you want to do?" I break my silence.

"Now, don't laugh," Dad looks at us sheepishly.

"Uh, ok?" Cameron answers him, but I'm not making any promises.

"I wanted to be a musician. I played guitar, and I was pretty good too. I was even writing my own songs. I told my father that was my dream and he hit the roof. He told me that I could join the military and be a man or pursue my flaky dream and be an embarrassment," Dad looks down at his wrinkled hands.

"Why didn't you get out, why did you go all the way to General?" I interrupt, twisting on the couch to face him straight on.

"I'm not sure, I guess once I was in the life, I figured I might as well do my best. After a few years, it got harder and harder to imagine leaving a steady job for my dream, so I figured I'd get as far as I could in my career."

"That makes sense," Cameron looks at me.

"The thing is, I always hoped one day that my father would take it back, you know about my music being an embarrassment. You both remember when Pops was in his last days, how I went to see him in the hospital," Dad looks up at our nodding faces. "He called me into his room and said, 'Don, there's something I need to tell you about your job,' and I thought that the moment had finally come." Dad stands up and walks over to the window before his emotions spill out. However, from where I'm sitting, I can see him wipe a tear away like a pesky mosquito that landed on his cheek.

"What did he say?" I ask.

"He told me that he was so proud of me for making it further than he ever did in the forces. He said I was a good man for following my calling," Dad sighs.

"Wow," Cameron crosses his arms across his chest.

"I didn't have the heart to tell him that I missed my calling. That my dream was music. Instead, I'd spent my life living his dream for me. He was old and frail, I didn't want to upset him," he explains.

"Do you regret that?" Cameron asks.

"Not telling him?" Dad answers, his back still to us as he stares out into the night.

"Yeah," Cameron stands up.

"No. I don't regret not telling him," Dad turns to face us and his eyes are glossy with tears threatening to fall. "I regret not pursuing the life that was meant to be mine," he wipes his fingers over his eyes, pushing away his emotions. "That's why I wanted to tell you boys, even though it's late, I wanted to tell you now that I'm proud of you for doing what's right for you. And, I hope you can forgive me," he hangs his head like a tired, old dog.

I jump to my feet and walk over to his side. Throwing my arms around him, I know I'm probably making my old man uncomfortable. Big hugs were never our thing. He's about to get even more uncomfortable though, as Cameron joins me in giving our elderly father a big bear hug.

"Of course, I forgive you," my brother whispers.

"It's water under the bridge, Dad," I agree. I give him a

squeeze and then let him go.

Dad looks up at us, his two little boys are all grown up now. Both of us towering over him.

"I love you boys, and I couldn't be more proud of you both."

"Thanks, Dad," I push down the growing lump in my throat, surprised by how much those words mean to me. How much I needed to hear them from him. "I love you too." I answer.

It's incredible to think of my father being a young man with a dream to play music. It's hard to imagine him forging a path that was never truly his. I've been uncertain about what I'm going to do after my own military career comes to a close. I might not have all the answers, but I know one thing, as long as I have the love and support of my family, I look from my big brother's face to my father's and smile, I can do anything.

CHAPTER 38

Jake

"So much for a quaint wedding," I look around the ballroom at the crowd of ridiculously built guys dressed in tuxes and suits.

"I think it's nice that Cameron's new teammates are here, it's a show of solidarity, right" Holly's beautiful blue eyes shine with happiness.

I'm not sure about what exactly happened between her and her parents, but I've never seen her so relaxed. She has always been gorgeous, but tonight in her deep green dress and with new life breathed into her, she's radiant. She looks like a princess from all of those fairy tales. If those princesses were innocent, sweet girls by day and wild vixens by night.

"Of course, you're right," I take a page from my brother's playbook about not arguing with your woman. I mean, sure Holly isn't pregnant or my fiancée, but that doesn't mean I can't fix both of those things. I let my eyes travel over her milky skin, savoring her low-cut dress. It isn't often I get to see her all dolled up, it's not like there were a lot of opportunities to put on our Sunday finest in rehab. I might just need to start upping my game, taking her out to some high society events, or at least crashing them. If it means I get to see her looking like this, then it's worth it.

Not that I mind seeing her any way. In sweats, cuddled up to me on the couch. Naked, with my throbbing cock between her fat lips. I groan and stir in my seat, trying to adjust for the unexpected, immediate effect that image had on my body.

God damn. I'm away from her for one night and I'm practically a horny teenager.

She's amazing.

"How about we dance?" She looks at me in a way that could convince me anything she's saying is worth doing. She could be asking me to run naked through an angry swarm of bees and I'd be stripping down without thought.

Dancing isn't the way I used to pick up the ladies. To say it's not my strong suit is a tragic understatement. Yet, I find myself pulling out her chair and offering her my arm as we make our way to the dance floor together. I'm not here to pick up ladies, I'm here to make the love of my life happy. Who cares if I can't dance? It's not about that.

The band is in the middle of playing another 'oldie but goodie' from God-knows-what era. I'm not certain, but I think any song that mentions 'the twist' is really more appropriate for a senior center's annual New Year's bash than a modern wedding. But what do I know?

"I'm not sure you can handle my sweet moves, I mean,

I'm not a professional dancer or anything, but you might find it hard to keep up," I tease her.

I lift my arms and try not to look like one of those inflatable tube-man balloons you see at car dealerships flailing about the discounted vehicles with my moves. From the look on Holly's face, I'm pretty sure I'm failing. Hard.

"Have you ever thought of doing Dancing with the Stars? I think they might just give it to you based on your audition alone," she laughs. I love her laugh, the music of it lifts my heart.

Thankfully, the song ends without me knocking Holly over or stepping on her white heels. We wait for the band to delve into the next song, but I stop in my tracks and stare at the stage as my father walks across it and whispers into the lead singer's ear.

What is he doing?

Dad and the man talk, nodding their heads and clearly coming to some kind of agreement. Then, the band puts down their instruments and leaves my father front and center.

I search the dance floor for Cameron. He's standing a few feet away from the stage with his brand-new wife on his arm, giving our father the same perplexed stare that I can feel pasted on my own face.

My father picks up one of the acoustic guitars the band left behind and makes his way to the mic. Now, this should be interesting. I can't look away. I can't blink. I don't want to miss whatever this is that's unfolding in front of my brother's wedding reception.

Dad leans into the mic too far and it sounds like thunder when he clears his throat. Ok, maybe I don't want to watch this. It's starting out like a train wreck. I search the room, pleading with my maker that no one is recording this on their phones. If my father is going to go down in flames, at least let him do it without it living forever on YouTube.

"Ahem," he clears his throat again, a look I've never seen is frozen on my father's face. He looks afraid. "I, uh, well, I asked the band if I could play a song and they graciously agreed," Dad holds up his hand to the retired band members sitting off to the side and the crowd claps uncertainly.

"What's he doing?" Holly whispers to me and I suddenly remember that she's standing next to me. I've been so focused on what is unfolding on the stage that the room around me almost disappeared.

"I couldn't tell ya," I answer with a shrug, never taking my eyes off of him.

"As you all know, my son Cameron married his beautiful bride, Chelsea today. Your mother and I couldn't be happier for you, Son. We couldn't have dreamed of a better daughter-in-law to welcome into our family," Dad looks down at my brother, smiling. "And God willing, perhaps we'll add another soon enough." My father gives me a little wink. Normally, I'd feel awkward with the public pressure. Tonight, I just return his relaxed smile. The old man and I haven't agreed on much over the years, but this is one time we see eye-to-eye.

"Aww, that's sweet," Holly rests her head on my shoulder softly and our fingers weave together as we listen.

"So, I wanted to come up here and give you guys a gift from the heart. I haven't sung publicly in over forty years, but I felt like this was the perfect special occasion to come out of hiding. This song is an old one, it's called 'Father and Son' by the artist known as Cat Stevens. He's since changed his name, but the meaning of this song never did. It's actually for both of my boys. Cameron, Jake, this one is for you," Dad looks down at the guitar in his hands and begins to strum the slow tune and the couples surge together on the dance floor.

I pull Holly into me, she leans her head against my chest and closes her eyes with a smile as we move in lazy circles around the dance floor.

I lean down and kiss Holly on her forehead, letting the moment wash over me. Letting myself feel it for once. Letting my emotions drown all the pain, the cynicism, the history. "Holly?" I murmur.

Dad's voice is rich and overflowing with emotions as he belts out the words that must speak to him like they were written for the sole purpose of him singing them.

A lump grows in my throat as I listen to my father sing the lyrics. His passion bleeds into every line, like he can finally express the lessons he's always wanted to teach us, but only through this song.

"I love you," my voice cracks and I pull her close.

"I love you too," she whispers.

We dance, listening to my father finally tell his sons the hopes and dreams he has for us. With the woman I never deserved dancing on the floor with me, I close my eyes, enjoying what feels like a dream. A dream that I never want to wake up from. This. Right here. This moment in time, it's perfect.

CHAPTER 39

Jake

The band has taken over the music once again, and we're back to swaying along to dated slow songs. Holly grinds her hips against mine, subtly at first, but when she looks up at me I can see from the twinkle in her eyes that she knows what she's doing.

"I was thinking," she purrs at me and my cock throbs instinctively at the desire coating her words, "maybe you and I should get out of here." Her painted lips twitch up into a coy smile.

Fuck, good luck getting all the way back to the hotel when she looks at me like that. I might just have to throw open the back door of the car and bend her over the seat. Maybe I'll just say the hell with privacy and fuck her out in the open, right on the hood.

"I think I could be convinced to go," I force my voice to remain nonchalant, despite how stiff she's made my cock. She doesn't need to know how with just a glance, she can reduce me to a hormonal teenaged boy all over again.

Holly slides her pussy across me, grinding into me without shame. So much for keeping a poker face. Her eyes light up as she feels the hard ridge of my shaft rub against her. "If that's how you're gonna play it," I grab her by the arm and lead her off the dance floor, "let's go." I'm not asking. Not that she's protesting. Her heels are clip-clopping on the floor as she struggles to keep up with my pace.

We walk out into the main hall and I look around at my options. I'm not taking her to the bathroom, it's too busy. My eyes glide down the hall and stop. I wordlessly circle my hand around her small wrist and guide her into the empty room.

The coat room is musty. The racks of unclaimed jackets surround us, reminding me of the forts I used to build with my brother as a child. It was incredible how long we could occupy ourselves with nothing but our imaginations and a blanket draped over a couple of chairs. It's so warm in here, I feel like stripping off this suit and leaving it in a puddle on the floor. I walk Holly to the back of the room, giving us a little shelter from anyone who might happen to glance in when they pass by.

I pull Holly into me so tight that you couldn't slip a sheet of paper between us, her blue eyes grow wide as she realizes my intentions. "We can't," she whispers unconvincingly. Her body is telling me a different story, her nipples are hard against her thin dress and her breathing is quick and shallow.

"Why not?" I smirk down at her.

"What if we get caught? What will people say?" She looks equally nervous and turned on. Wasn't she the one who once told me you can't be scared and horny at the same time? I guess I need to give her a reason to forget her fear.

"Fuck social graces," I growl. "I'm going to take you right here, right now."

I feel her thighs squeeze together, and the scent of her desire floods my nostrils. I consider tearing her dress from her body, but my better sense kicks in and reminds me that she still needs to leave the coat room once I'm done with her. The thought of fucking her in such a risky, public place has me rock hard.

Holly bites her bottom lip and looks up at me from under her heavy lashes. My cock throbs with need, begging me to push her to her knees and make her wrap her lips around me. I manage to pry my eyes away and check the room once more to make sure we're still alone. Hidden behind two sprawling coatracks, we're well concealed, despite the wide-open door. Pushing her back against the wall, I devour her mouth in a fiery kiss as I push her billowy skirt up her legs and over her hips.

Holly moans into my mouth, opening her stance a little, allowing me to easily thrust my hand into her soaking panties where my fingers are instantly coated with her nectar. I slide my finger across her eager slit and plunge it inside her quivering pussy, feeling like I might explode as she grips her inside muscles against me. She's so tight. All of my restraint disappears, and I unstrap my belt, pulling open my pants in a flurry. "Face the wall," my voice is like gravel across my vocal chords.

She looks uncertain as she peers over at the door, but I don't have the patience for second-guessing now. Grabbing her hips firmly in my hands, I flip her in one effortless swoop, pushing her against the wall. She gasps loudly, but doesn't refuse my advances, instead she pushes her hands against the wall like a criminal about to be patted down by an officer and wiggles her supple ass at me like a cat twitching its tail.

"That's my good girl, you're loving this, aren't you? Tell me what you want me to do to you," I demand.

"I want to feel you," she begs me, but it's not enough. After the way she was teasing me, testing me, it's my turn.

"Feel me what?" I wrap my hand up in her beautiful curls she did just for the wedding and yank her head back to me.

"To feel you fuck me, hard," her voice is strained with desire.

Pulling my cock from my boxers, I hook my arm around her waist and pull her ass toward me until her back is flat like a tabletop and her eager pussy is waiting for my cock. Grabbing her thong, I twist it in my hand until the elastic and lace give way, exploding across my fist in a painful snap. "Ow! Hey, those were expensive!" She complains, looking over her shoulder back at me.

"If you keep making a fuss, I'll have to put them in your mouth," I growl. Her eyes widen, but she arches her back and grinds her firm ass over my thick cock in approval. I grab a foil packet from my wallet and quickly rip it open with my teeth, my eyes never leaving her round ass. I roll the condom down to the base and sink myself inside her quivering pussy in one long thrust, filling her with my girth as she moans so loud that I'm certain anyone standing within ten feet of the door can hear her.

I already dropped her snapped thong on the floor, so I can't make good on my threat to stuff it in her mouth. Instead, I give her ass a sharp slap, and she bears down on my cock as I slide it inside her until my hips thrust against her shapely ass. She moans again, and I cover her mouth with my hand, not because I'm afraid of what people will say if we get caught, but because I'm not willing to have this moment stolen from me by some nosy intruder.

This time, she grunts much quieter than before. Although her body is telling me what her restricted moaning can't, she wants it hard. Holding each of her hips like a handle I pull almost all the way out and plunge into her core again and again.

She twists her ass, pushing back against me every time I bottom out inside her, giving me the deepest access possible to her center. Reaching around her hips, I make quick work of finding her sensitive nub hidden in her mound. I move my finger in little circles, easily sliding with her natural lubricant dripping on my fingertip. Suddenly, she stops moving, her pussy clenches and trembles around my cock, milking it for my seed as she slaps her hand over her own mouth and stifles her growing cries. There's no mistaking when this woman is cumming, if her body doesn't tell you loud enough, her muffled screams will.

My balls tighten as I slam my cock into her faster. With her muscles bearing down on me, she feels as tight as a virgin against my thick girth. A white wave of pure bliss flashes through my body as I cum. When the last tremors stop and I've emptied my seed, I lean over her, both of us gasping to catch our breaths.

I stand up straight and carefully remove the condom, tying it off at the top. I look around the room and see a wastepaper basket and toss it in. Holly composes herself, smoothing her dress back down over her ass. Although, it's a damned shame that she should cover it. Within a minute, we're both squared away.

"You ready to go back out?" I look down at her peaceful smile. If I didn't know that she was sober, I'd think that she was buzzing pretty good right now. Her cheeks are flush and her eyes are twinkling like she's just thrown back a couple of glasses of wine.

"Do you think anyone heard us?" She whispers nervously.

I shrug, "Fuck 'em. I don't care about what anyone in this world thinks, besides you," I admit quietly. Holly's smile spreads and her shoulders relax as the tension slides out of them.

"Ok, I'm ready," she laces her fingers in mine and we head out of the coat room with much less urgency than when we came in.

Walking out the door, I realize that Holly's torn thong is still on the floor by the back wall. A smile pulls at my lips as I imagine seeing the janitor's reaction as he finds them. It's either something he's used to discovering after every wedding reception, or it'll be his lucky day with a find like that. Either way, I don't care.

I lean down and softly kiss Holly on her forehead. Every day is my lucky day as long as I have this amazing woman by my side.

CHAPTER 40

Jake

"That was amazing," Holly looks up at me coyly and I wrap my arm around her shoulders, pulling her in for a kiss.

"You're amazing," I answer honestly.

What did I ever do to deserve a woman so warm, so beautiful, and so fucking sexy? I'm not sure that I ever deserved this angel that dropped into my lap, but I'll do whatever is within my power to keep her there.

"Are you ready to head out? It's been a long day," she tilts her head and her long hair flows down her arm, "I'd kinda like to get back to the hotel room and maybe relax in the tub for a bit," a sly smile spreads across her face.

I trail my fingers over the back of her neck and pull her tight against me, looking down at her sultry lips, "Is that right?" I murmur. "Maybe I'll join you, I'm pretty sure I can ease away all your tension." I run my other hand down her back and dig my fingers into her plump ass, making her gasp before I cover her lips with my kiss.

Our tongues collide feverishly, like they're desperate to be reunited. I can taste her passion, her desire, her eternal longing on her tongue. I have half a mind to drag her back into the coat closet for another round, but as she pulls back and looks up at me with those sweet baby blues, I know I want to take her back to our room so I can claim her as mine again and again. I want to savor every inch of her as I make her cry out my name until her throat is so raw she can't speak. I want to make her cum until she crumples with exhaustion. I want to lie in bed with her with our flesh pressed together as one, our limbs tied together in a true lover's knot that neither of us will be eager to untie.

"I'm ready to go," I growl, hungry for another taste of her. "I just…" I search my mind for what it is I was supposed to do. All rational thoughts have been stripped away from me, replaced by my one primal instinct to rip off Holly's clothes and make her mine.

"Are you going to say goodbye to your brother?" She throws me a lifeline, saving me from drowning in my lust.

"That's it," I snap my fingers. "Let's go wish them well and then we can get out of here." I run my fingers over the side of her rosy cheek and tilt her chin up as I smother her delicate lips with another kiss.

I step back and hold out my hand to her, but she doesn't take it. "If it's ok with you, I'd like to get some fresh air," she smiles. "Someone's got me all worked up and I need to cool down."

"Ok, well don't let yourself get too cool. I have plans for you later," I let my gaze slide over her curves, shamelessly enjoying every detail. "I'll be out in a minute," I let go of her hand and watch as she walks toward the front door. The hypnotic sway of her hips, the jiggle of her round ass against the flimsy fabric of her dress. I have to force myself to walk away.

I quickly make it back into the ballroom, on a mission to track down my brother as quickly as possible so I can get back to Holly.

Twisting my head like an owl, I scan the room for his familiar face. Finally, I spot him off to the side of the dance floor, talking with Dad. I hurry over to them, not caring if I'm interrupting a moment. I've got other things on my mind.

"There he is," Dad looks up at me. "Were your ears burning?"

"No, why? Were you talking about me?" I look from my father's face to my brother's.

"I was just telling Cameron how proud I am of you boys. It's incredible to watch your children grow up. To see you become men that I couldn't admire more." He looks over at my brother, "You'll know soon enough what it's like. Enjoy them while they're young. Everyone says it, but it's so easy to forget. One day your little one will be sleeping against your chest and the next they'll be off to college. Or having kids of their own," Dad smiles wistfully.

"I will," Cameron answers. He turns his attention to me, "I suppose that you're next," he beams at me knowingly.

"How's that?" I try to guess at the meaning of his words.

"We were just saying that we'll all be doing this again

soon," Cameron sweeps his hand over the room full of family and friends. "I can see from the way you look at Holly that there's going to be another wedding in our future."

"I don't know about that," I shrug it off, but inside his words cling to my heart. I've never made any plans to propose, the whole 'taking it one day at a time' thing has really been the main focus. However, I realize that Cameron has vocalized what my gut has been telling me since I first met Holly.

She's the one.

"Well, wedding or not, I'm just happy to see you've both found wonderful women that make you happy," Dad looks at us.

"Thanks, Pops," I answer.

"Hey, I wanted to let you know that I'm heading out. This was the perfect start to an amazing life for you, bro," I look at my big brother. "I can't wait to watch you play your season, and I can't wait to meet your little one when the time comes. You've got a big year ahead of you, and it couldn't happen to a more deserving guy." I grab my brother's hand and give it a shake, but pull him in for a hug.

"Thanks, Jake," he throws his arm around me tight. "That means a lot to me coming from you, man."

I step back and look over at my father, "Are we good, Pops?" I tilt my head and watch him slowly nod.

"We're good. Always," he throws his arms around me and gives me a strong squeeze. The man might be getting older, but his strength is still there.

I clap his back and step back smiling. Clearing my

throat, I push down the emotions threatening to spill out of me. "All right!" I say too loudly to mask the tremble in my voice, "I'll see you soon, I hope," I nod at Dad and he agrees. "And you, have fun on your honeymoon. Give me a call when you're back," I look at Cameron.

"Will do," he agrees.

I don't drag it out anymore, instead I head back out to the hall and stride toward the front doors of the building, hypnotically drawn to Holly's light that I can't see through the door, but I know is there. Like a moth to a flame.

"Ahhhh! Noooo! Lemme go!"

My blood turns cold as Holly's screams reverberate against the walls. My heart pounds in my chest twice as fast as my feet hit the floor. I bolt for the door.

"Help!" She shrieks.

I fling the front door open and scan the darkness for her. Where is she? Oh God, where is she?

"Holly!" I yowl out into the darkness like a wolf calling out to the moon. "Holly! I'm coming!"

CHAPTER 41

Holly

"Shut the fuck up!" Knox backhands me across my cheek and my head whips over to the side. A trickle of blood flows from my split lip leaving a taste of salty copper on my tongue. I twist and thrash against him, but I can't break loose from his iron grip. Knox drags me like a rag doll out into the dark parking lot, away from the building. Away from Jake. Away from any chance of escape.

Terror bubbles up inside me and I flail erratically like a fish dangling on a line. "Help!" I scream as loud as I can, desperate for anyone to hear. I was just standing at the bottom of the steps, looking up at the stars and thinking of how incredibly blessed I am, literally moments ago. Then I felt a tight squeeze around my neck as Knox wrapped his arm around my throat, clamping his hand down over my mouth and dragged me away.

"Holly?" I can hear Jake back at the building.

Knox yanks a gun from the back of his pants and cocks

it against my temple. "Go ahead, call out to your perfect Prince Charming," he sneers. "I'll empty your brains right here on the pavement, and then his," he twists me around to face him and I can see the gleeful glint in his wild eyes daring me to challenge him. To give him a reason.

Somehow, I manage to swallow my instinct to cry out, frozen in a headlock against Knox's arm with a gun to my head. I wish this wasn't a familiar feeling.

"Ahh, you always were my good girl, weren't you," he jerks his arm tighter across my throat and begins to drag me away. For the first time, I notice he doesn't have the same swagger he used to. His leg bounces with every step as he pulls me further from Jake. He's walking with a limp.

It feels like a lifetime ago that I shot him. Clearly, not to him. Knox is the kind of man who seldom forgets and never forgives.

I fight to push away the woozy feeling that's surrounding me. I can barely breathe with Knox's choke hold twisted around my neck. The stars begin to blend together and swirl, like a Van Gogh painting, as the world begins to feel fuzzy around the edges. I can't feel my feet and my arms are taken over by pins and needles, my vision is starting to tunnel.

"Holly!" Jake's voice sounds so distant. Like a memory or a dream.

Knox stops beside a black Cadillac and flings the trunk up. He finally releases my neck and shoves me toward the opening. "Get in, bitch. You and I have so much catching up to do. I can't wait to get started." He throws me against the cold, hard metal edge of the open trunk and I cling onto the sides, fighting to keep my legs rooted to the ground.

"Jake! Over here!" I scream, twisting myself sideways in an attempt to break free. Knox grabs a fistful of my hair, using it to control my head as he pins me under him. He plunges my face into the darkness of the trunk, leaving my ass hanging over the back edge. I can feel him grind his filthy cock against my ass as he runs the cold steel of his gun up the inside of my trembling thighs.

"Yeah, we've got lots of catching up to do." I can hear him behind me. He pushes the nozzle of his gun flat against my pussy and panicked tears choke me. I sob into the trunk, at his mercy. And Knox has no mercy.

"Once I'm done fucking every hole on your tight little body, I'm gonna shoot it. First, I'll shoot your asshole, then your pussy, I'll save your mouth for last so you don't die too quick. I'm gonna enjoy letting you bleed out like the fucking pig you are," Knox crushes me against the edge of his trunk, his body weight flattening me, making the metal edge dig underneath my ribs and push the air from my lungs.

I'm crying so hard, but I can't pull the oxygen I need into my body. I start to cough and sputter.

I have no doubt, none whatsoever, that he will make good on his promises. If I don't die here first.

"Knox, get the fuck away from her," Jake's voice booms from behind me. It bounces off the inside of the trunk, like an echo in a cave, reassuring me.

"Fuck you," I hear Knox spit at him and am suddenly free as his body is plucked from mine.

I stand up and gasp for air, whirling around to see Jake pounce on Knox like a starving lion taking down a sickly hyena.

"You think you're a badass because you beat down a woman?" Jake rolls on top of him. "I've taken out the biggest terrorist in the fucking world. You're nothing but a little bitch," He punches Knox in the face and his head flings back against the pavement.

I don't know what to do other than watch in horror as they struggle for control of the gun. Knox isn't nearly as big as Jake, but he's like a weasel. He's able to maintain control of the weapon as he twists out of the way of Jake's heavy punch. His hand hits the cement with a sickening thud and a smile slicks across Knox's face as Jake grimaces in pain.

I look around frantically. I don't have a phone to call 9-1-1. I can't see anyone by the building or out in the parking lot, but I can't just stand here like a fool. I start screaming my head off for help.

"Please, help! Anyone! Call the cops! Help!" I shriek desperately.

Jake balls up his fist again, but this time he doesn't miss Knox's sharp nose. Blood explodes from his face as his nose is mangled under the force of Jake's punch. I watch as Knox's eyes roll back into his head with wonder. Did Jake knock him out?

Jake twists Knox's hands, trying to pluck the gun from him, but he can't. Under him, Knox is still managing to cling to the weapon, pointing it at Jake's face.

"Please! Help! Oh my God, he's going to kill him! Help!" I break down into hysterics, but no one is coming.

The two men writhe on the ground, yanking for control of the gun. Knox points it at Jake, then Jake takes control and aims it at Knox. My heart is beating out of my chest and I can't stop screaming at the top of my lungs, feeling like a helpless, pathetic, fool.

BANG!

I watch in horror as Jake slumps over Knox. "Oh my god! No!" I cry out, running over to Jake. I don't care anymore what happens to me. If Jake is dead, I have nothing left to live for.

I throw my arms over Jake's shoulders and he slides off of Knox's body before standing up, gun in hand.

He's alive! I look down to the pavement at the blood gushing from Knox's chest. There's no doubt from the hole in his body that he's not walking away from this one.

"I thought he killed you. I thought," I throw my arms around Jake's neck and he lifts me up, swirling me around and gives me a kiss.

"Are you ok?" His eyes are full of concern as he gently puts me back on my feet and rubs his thumb over my fat lip.

"It's nothing," I grab his hand and look him over, still not fully convinced that he wasn't hurt somehow. "I'm just so glad you're ok. I'm so glad it's over," the words tumble out of my mouth.

I look over to the front of the building, Cameron and his father are running out the doors toward us. My eyes fall back to Knox's lifeless body bleeding out the same way he wanted me to.

"It's over," Jake reassures me, running his swollen hand over my hair. "It's over." He pulls me into his chest and I listen to his heartbeat, shaking as my nerves try to settle.

I can't believe that Knox is dead. That I'm finally free.

Forever. I cling to the only man I've ever truly loved. The man who just saved my life. My hero. I listen to his heart promising me of our days to come. Of our freedom. Of our future. Of a life without Knox.

   I'm finally free.

CHAPTER 42

Jake

"Am I going to jail? It was self-defense!" I can feel myself getting worked up as the detective finally comes back into the room. He's left me sitting here for at least an hour. Do they think I'm lying? I should probably call a lawyer. This whole night has been so chaotic, I haven't been thinking straight. I should've demanded a lawyer an hour ago.

"Petty Officer Armstrong, please, calm down." The officer casually strolls across the room, his ginger hair brightening under the fluorescent lights above. The hues of orange and red remind me of campfires we had when I was a kid. Except now, instead of roasting marshmallows and telling ghost stories, I might be getting my ass roasted while I live the craziest horror story of all.

"How can you tell me to calm down? You've left me here forever. I think I should get a lawyer," I search his pale, freckled face for answers, but I can't read him.

"You are free to call a lawyer, if you want. However, I

think you should probably put that off for the time being," he plops down in the seat across the table from me, lying his beige folder down in front of him.

"Why is that?" I squint my eyes, trying to zero in on some kind of tell, some facial twitch, some movement that would give me an idea of what's going on behind his stony face.

"That you won't call your lawyer?" His voice is monotone. It's driving me crazy.

"Yes."

"Well, it's simple math really. You're going to be free to go in about five minutes. I believe your lawyer," he checks his wristwatch with a smarmy smile, "would probably take close to another hour to get here. So, my best guess is that you'll forgo the lawyer and just go home." His face cracks into a smile. It's a welcome change. Even if it is a smug smile.

"I'm free to go?" I look down at the folder he still hasn't cracked the cover on.

"You sure are," he nods.

"What's going to happen? Am I going to trial?" I try to figure out what the months ahead are going to bring.

"Listen, you called it self-defense, right?" He locks his brown eyes on mine and I wordlessly confirm with a nod. "Well, around here we call it the 'Stand Your Ground' law. You were under attack, your life was in danger, so it was you or him. So far, between your story and your girlfriend's account of the whole thing synchronizing perfectly and the fact that our dearly deceased has been a most wanted criminal in this state for over five years, it's looking like an open and shut case," he explains patiently.

I breathe a deep sigh of relief as a weight I hadn't even realized I was carrying, lifts from my soul. "That's great," I smile.

"Now, don't get me wrong, it's not shut yet. We just found out that the parking lot where this unfortunate event took place has security cameras installed. We're going to examine the footage, of course, and make sure it corroborates what you've told us," he looks down at his folder and then back up at me, "which we expect it will."

"Ok, great. So, I can go home. Like, head back to Virginia Beach tomorrow? Or, how does that work?" I fold my fingers together and try not to look too damned happy right now.

"Yes, you can go back home tomorrow. And as to whether or not this will go to trial, I'm not really supposed to make a call on that. However, if the footage backs up your story, I can't see this going past the pre-hearing judge. My guess is, you'll be granted immunity."

"Ok, that's great." Try as I might, I can't keep the smile from spreading across my face. After all we've been through, after all Knox put Holly through, it's hard not to feel good about him being wiped off the earth.

"Ok, so I'm going to need your John Hancock on some paperwork and then you'll be free to go. We're also discharging your girl, so you guys can leave together."

"Thank you so much." I hold out my hand to Officer Houston and he gives it a firm shake.

"No problem," he cracks the cover on his folder and pulls out a stack of papers. "Before we get to these, I want to tell you that you should consider yourself a hero. What you did tonight was nothing short of heroic, you saved your girl and you took a good-for-nothing thug with a rap sheet longer than my arm, off our streets. You can walk out of here with your head held high," he doesn't blink as he stares me down.

"Thank you," my voice drops. The last time someone told me I was a hero for the kill shot I made, I felt like a monster. This time, under these circumstances, it feels good. "That means a lot to me," I admit. "Thank you."

"Thank you," he emphasizes, finally dropping his intense gaze to the paperwork. "Ok, I won't take up anymore of your time than I have to. Let's get this stuff signed and you'll be free to walk out of here." He smiles and pulls a pen out of his dress shirt, tossing it across the table at me.

"Perfect," I click the pen and grab the first sheet from the top of the stack. "Ok, where do I sign?"

CHAPTER 43

Holly

My shoes squeak against the floor as I make my way down the hall. I've been a wreck all night. Almost being kidnapped by Knox, then watching a man who has controlled my life for years finally meet the fate I've dreamt about for months; it's been a lot to process.

I can't wait to get out of here and see Jake again. I just want to feel his arms around me, I want him to tell me this is all over. To hear him say that it's all going to be all right. I run my own hand down the length of my hair, thinking about how soothing it feels when he does it. It's a poor substitute for the comfort he brings me.

I follow the officer guiding me through the halls out to the main entrance. Waiting there, watching the door like a hawk, is my man. He looks so handsome as the worry on his face dissolves into happiness at the sight of me. That look that's on his face right now. The one that's about as close to pure joy as you can get without drugs or sex, that's because of me. It's an amazing feeling to know someone loves you that much.

"Holly!" He closes the gap between us and wraps his thick arms around me. "Are you ok?" Concern clouds over his sky blue eyes as he looks me over.

"I'm fine, I just want to go home," I admit.

"Let's get back to the hotel," Jake agrees, "it's been a long night."

He holds out the crook of his arm, like a gentleman and I lace my own arm through it, exiting the station at his side.

As soon as we walk through the doors, I can hear my mother, "There she is! They're out now," I scan the crowd of faces seeing Jake's parents, his brother and Chelsea, and wedged amongst them are my parents.

"How did you?" I search my mind for answers, "how did you know?" I ask my mother as she races over to my side.

"Jake's mother called me, we jumped in the car and drove like a bat out of hell to get here. Oh, my goodness! Look at your face!" Tears spring in Mom's eyes. "Are you ok? She wraps her arms around me and kisses my cheek.

"I am, I promise," I reassure her.

"Give the girl some room, Beverly," Dad cuts in and my mom takes a small step back. My father steps up to Jake, toe-to-toe, and looks him straight in the eyes, he thrusts his hand out to him and gives Jake a vigorous handshake. "I can't thank you enough. I'm so glad she never listened to us. We didn't take it seriously enough when you guys said she was in danger," my father rambles, "but you were right. You saved my little girl." Dad's voice cracks and his eyes well up, "Thank you."

"I would do it again in a heartbeat," Jake looks over at me. I know he's not lying. Jake has told me from the beginning that he would always keep me safe. Tonight, he proved exactly to what lengths he'll go to in order to keep his word.

"I'm so happy you're ok," Mom sobs and my father holds her tight as her tears spill down onto his shirt. "I don't know what I would've done if something had happened to you," she wails.

"Shhh, she's ok. You don't need to think about that," Dad soothes her.

Jake's family surrounds him, telling him how proud they are of him and his mother is bawling just as hard as mine is. It's a lot to try to come to terms with. If the trigger had been pulled while Knox still had control of the gun, our mothers would be crying their eyes out for a very different reason right now.

Jake pulls away from his family, "I'm sorry guys, I gotta do something right now. It can't wait," he explains and walks over to me. He pulls me away from my parents, firmly planting a hand on each of my shoulders and looks down into my eyes. God, those eyes. I could get lost in the hypnotic blue forever.

I slap both my hands over my mouth, wincing with the pain of my forgotten split lip, but right now, I don't give a shit about that. Jake slides down, settling on one knee in front of my and our families collectively gasp along with me.

"Holly, never has it been clearer what I want to do with my life, than right now. Tonight, I almost lost you," he looks down and shakes his head and I place my hand softly on his shoulder. Jake clears his throat and presses on, "I could've lost you, but I didn't. I know that I never want to spend another day of my entire life without you in it. I don't have a ring to give you right now, but I still want to humbly ask you, will you be my wife?"

"Here, borrow mine," Chelsea slides her engagement ring off her finger, putting her wedding ring back in place. She holds it out to Jake and he grasps the gold band with the extravagant diamond, holding it up to me.

"Thank you, Chelsea," his voice is so full of emotion, it's amazing he can talk. It's more than I can say for myself. My words won't even squeak out past my tight vocal chords.

I nod my head as tears stream down my face and hold out my trembling hand to him. "Y-yes," I somehow make the word fall out of my mouth.

Jake slides Chelsea's ring onto my finger and stands back up, sliding his arms around me, he dips me back dramatically and softly covers my swollen lip with a kiss. I can hear our families clapping around us as I melt into his strong arms. I can't imagine a more intense, or a more perfect proposal. Jake is the only man I've ever truly loved, and now I get to show him that for the rest of our lives. This feels like a dream, only better.

It's a dream come true.

CHAPTER 44

Jake

"Let's get cleaned up," I walk into the hotel bathroom and run the water into the tub. I mess around with the taps until the water is just right, then search through the array of mini soaps and bottles on a little platter by the sink. I don't even know what half of these things are. What the hell is a body butter? I finally spot the bubble bath and squeeze the entire pearly goop into the bath, swishing it around until it foams up.

"Sounds great, are you gonna join me?" Holly yells from the other room.

"Of course."

She appears in the doorway with a smile that could light up the night's sky. I don't have a chance to utter a word, I can't stop studying every inch of her. My gaze slides down to the sparkling ring on her finger. She's mine. The thought gives me a jolt of pride and I stand a little taller. This amazing woman is all mine.

"Get over here," I reach my hand out to her and she grasps it with her dainty fingers. Pulling her into me, I lean over her and watch as she flutters her eyes closed, waiting for my kiss. I drag my thumb down the side of her face and lace my fingers through the back of her hair, bringing her lips to mine. I'm careful not to hurt her split lip, the last injury she will ever suffer at the hands of that fucking piece of shit, Knox. May he burn in hell.

I trail quick kisses across her jawbone and over to her ear. Holly moans loudly as I pull her soft earlobe into my mouth and flicker it lightly with my tongue.

I feel her body surrender to me, relaxing in my arms as she tilts her head toward my mouth. I breathe against her sensitive neck, letting the hot air billow around her skin and whisper in her ear, "I love you."

"Mmm, I love you too," she murmurs.

"Turn around," I demand. She does what I ask, she's my good girl. I slide the zipper on the back of her gown down until it stops just above her ass. The dress peels open, revealing her creamy skin to me. I glide my fingers under the edges, guiding them over her shoulders and helping them down over her arms until her dress is barely clinging to her hips like a hula skirt. Holly shakes her plump ass and the illusion is shattered as the dress crumples at her feet.

I can't move, I'm transfixed by my woman, my fiancée, standing before me like a goddess. She gasps and quickly goes over to the tub, twisting the taps until the water is nothing more than a couple of drops falling into the full bath.

"You get in first," I tell her.

She nods. I hold her hand as she gracefully steps into

the water. I watch as she eases down into the tub, sliding beneath the rainbow-colored bubbles. She lays back and flutters her eyes closed as she lets the stress of the last few hours soak away.

I can't take my eyes off of her. She's still my beautiful contradiction. In moments like this, she looks so innocent. So untouched by the terrible pain that she's suffered. It amazes me that someone as tiny and as sweet as Holly has grieved the losses she has and endured the torture she's been subjected to.

Never again. She's mine now and I'll do everything I can to give her the life she's never had. The life she truly deserves. One filled with love, happiness, and pleasure.

"You're safe now, just like I promised," I look down at her.

Holly opens her eyes and smiles despite the tears threatening to fall. "I know. For the first time since," she tilts her head and thinks, "well, since I was a kid. Since before Heather died, I really believe that. I finally feel safe. Like I can begin again. Like we can start a new life, together." She wipes away her tears. "Now, get in here with me. I'm lonely without you," She pleads with me.

I quickly strip out of my dress shirt and pants, the tie and jacket were long ago abandoned. I step into the warm water behind Holly and shift myself so she's cradled in my arms and between my legs.

"You know, I've been thinking about what I want to do after my contract expires," I cup warm water in my hand and let it fall over her hair.

"Really," she relaxes back against me, "what's that?"

"I think I'd like to use my veteran's education benefit to get into social work, maybe even addiction counseling,"

I admit. "I used to think it was all a bunch of bullshit, the counseling thing, you know? Like, how could a bunch of talking help you get over anything? But, look at us," I smile down at her.

"Look at us," she agrees as she reaches up and runs her hand over my beard.

"It completely changed our lives. I want to be a part of that for someone else, you know? I want to help other people the same way I was helped. Cause, if they can even find a fraction of the happiness I've found," I lean into her and she twists around so I can kiss her softly, "then that's a career worth having."

"I think you'll be a great counselor," Holly smiles up at me.

"I hope you realize that we'll both be students at the same time," I warn her.

"Yeah, so?"

"Well, I just hope you know that when you agreed to marry me, you were agreeing to years of eating ramen noodles and cheap date nights," I tease her. "And it's too late to take it back," I laugh.

"I don't want you to take it back," she giggles. "And I don't care if we do have to eat ramen or any of that, if I have you, that's all I need," she squirms up against me and kisses my cheek.

She knows what she's doing, the way she's wiggling her ass against my cock, grinding into me like a dirty girl all while looking at me with wide-eyed innocence.

I groan and pull her tight against me as my cock grows rigid against the crack of her ass. "It's too bad we took this bath," I growl.

"Why is that," she bats her eyelashes at me, toying with me as she rubs herself against my hard cock.

"Because with all of the dirty things I'm about to do to you, you're going to need another one in a couple of hours," I stand up and my cock sways slightly. Holly looks at my girth with truly wide eyes now.

I lean over and grab her hands, lifting her easily to her feet. I step out of the tub and then effortlessly lift her into my arms like the bride she has agreed to be and carry her across the threshold into our hotel bedroom.

Holly squeals as I drop her down onto the bed and I immediately jump on, covering her with my body. She's mine, for now and forever, we might not have walked down the aisle today, but I'm going to fuck her like it's our wedding night. Tonight is our new beginning, our fresh start. Tonight, will be one she's never going to forget.

EPILOGUE

Jake

"It's hard to believe that it's already been ten years since I graduated from here on this very stage," I look out into the crowded auditorium at the latest inpatients working through Edgewood's program. I remember the mandatory attendance at cake nights all too well. When we had to sit through speeches from former addicts and patients of the program who were celebrating months and even years of sobriety. When I sat in those seats, I was never fully convinced I'd ever be back to celebrate my own success.

"It feels like it was a lifetime ago that I walked through these halls," I look down into the front row to Holly's smiling face. Next to her, our beautiful five-year-old daughter is grinning up at me proudly. Her long blonde hair is glowing under the fluorescent lights, making her look like the angel she is.

It was important to Holly that we name her after her sister, Heather. From what her parents say, the name suits her just fine. A quiet, smart girl, always quick to laugh or throw her arms around you in a freakishly strong hug for such a little thing. Apparently, she's a lot like the aunt she was named after.

"In some ways," I wink at my little girl, already in kindergarten and growing up too fast, "it was a lifetime ago."

I look down at the notes I've made on my phone, resting on the podium. When I was asked to come back here, I came up with a big speech, but now, it just feels all wrong. I stuff my phone in my pocket and clear my throat.

Looking over at the aging faces of the counselors still working here, I remember how I once spent my time scowling at them. I smile at Ms. Morehouse. Hell, I even give Gavin a smirk, although I'm not fully convinced he's happy to see me.

Filling my lungs full of air, I peer out into the crowd and give my head a shake. It's time to speak from the heart.

"Listen, I had a big plan to tell you about how well my life is going now that I'm sober. And, it's true. I found the one woman on this earth who makes me happier to be alive just by waking up next to her in the morning. She gave me an amazing daughter who gives each day of my life meaning. I went to school and am now working in a career I love, helping veterans who suffer from addiction issues. I have all of this now, and I was really excited to share that with you. To tell you how it's all possible, if you stay sober, if you follow your plan, and if you don't give up." I scan the crowd, my eyes settling on faces that could've been mine a decade ago. The sour looks of cynicism and doubt.

"But, you know what?" I stare out at them, remembering all too well how it felt to be in their shoes. "None of that matters to you. It's not a promise that you're going to leave here and find someone who makes your life whole. There's no guarantee that you're going to experience the joy of children, or even be forgiven by the children some of you already have." The audience murmurs and people begin to shuffle in their seats. I look down at Holly and watch her beautiful blue eyes grow wide with surprise.

"What are you doing?" She mouths the words at me.

"Nobody is promised a beautiful future unless they put the work into the present," I continue. "When I first walked through the doors of this building ten years ago, well sauntered in is more like it," I chuckle, "I thought this place was a spa." A ripple of laughter fills the room.

"Oh, come on, I know I'm not the only one who thought that. Admit it, some of you came in here with your golf clubs ready or wondering where the pool was, right?"

I see the nodding heads in the crowd. The twinkle in their eyes as they agree with me.

"Well, that was me too. I figured this was a joke and for a long time, that's how I treated it. And guess what? I went home from here and I relapsed the first time I was met with temptation," I hit my fist against the podium. "I messed up," I look down into Holly's eyes still feeling the guilt swirl up inside me all these years later for the pain I caused her that day.

Holly's eyes are brimming with tears, and she pulls our daughter in closer to her side. I force myself to look away, to find my words, to focus.

"I may have fallen down that day, but the important thing…the life changing thing, is that I got back up. I remembered what I was taught here and I persevered. It wasn't always easy to stay sober. There were many more tough times. Times when I was tempted. Times when I wanted nothing more than to go back to drugs and forget the pain, but I walked through it. I was forged by the fire that tried to destroy me, it made me stronger and if you don't give up, if you take this seriously, if you do the work now, you'll be stronger too." I take a deep breath and look down at my wife and my baby girl.

My heart swells in my chest, "don't focus on your failures. Celebrate your victories, no matter how small. Be grateful for the things you have, even when it's less than what others have. Maybe you won't have kids, maybe you don't want to. Maybe you won't go back to school. It doesn't matter if you do, really. All that matters is that you don't give up. I might not be able to promise you the same happiness that's touched my life, but I can promise you that you'll find your own."

I swallow the hard lump threatening to break my voice and look down at my family. The family I never thought I'd find. The family I never thought I deserved. The family that gave me back a life worth living.

"You'll only be able to live your best life tomorrow by putting the work in now. So, to all of you who have been sitting through tonight with sighs and eye-rolling, believe me, I was once you. I know you don't think there's anything out there for you. You're wrong. Believe in yourself and, I promise you, it gets better. So much better than you can even imagine right now," my voice cracks as Heather and Holly smile up at me.

"I love you, Daddy!" Heather cries out. The crowd collectively "ahhhs" and a few people clap.

"I love you too, honey. I love you both. So much." I look back up at the unfamiliar faces in the crowd and nod, "Thank you for listening." I glance over at the counselors at the side of the stage, "Thank you for giving me back my life," I choke on the emotion in my voice. My eyes travel back down into the front row to my girls in their pastel blue dresses, "Thank you for giving me the best ten years any man could dream of." I wipe the tear threatening to fall from my eye down my cheek and leave the podium.

The auditorium erupts in cheers and clapping, but I don't look back. Forward is the only direction I look now, each day being brighter than the last.

Each day, a gift.

Made in the USA
Charleston, SC
25 January 2017